To all of those who help

CW00859649

To those who tore it (

To those who supported me when I felt like I couldn't go on.

To those of you who inspired me with their own literary creations.

And to all of those in the writing community who welcomed me as one of their own.

My love, my respect and my thanks.

TEMPLE WOOD

JENS FARM

THE GLEN

KILMICHAEL

DUNADD

CAIRNBAAN

ACHNABREAC

EDWOSE

☆: Cists
⊙ : Circles
x : Stones

Prologue

The Voice.

Once again whispering in his mind. It had been silent for years, longer than years and yet, last night as he lay, trying to sleep, it had come to him. It was time. He'd known for a while now. It was time to finish what they had started all those years ago. He understood now, could view things that had happened in the past with the clarity of hindsight. There could be no ending, so long as he stayed here.

He paused on the hilltop, breathing heavily. The view down the glen was as he remembered it. There were more trees, there was a little more noise, but it was essentially the same. Change had come here slowly. Grudgingly. This was a place of stories. Of legend. It was etched into the very rocks, into the standing stones which littered the valley. He could see them there, standing tall and silent. Their song long since faded. History had made its home here and on days like this he could feel it reaching out to claim him.

Wearily he leaned on his staff, age comes to us all, eventually. Even to one such as he. 76 Years old. Never would he have thought it. The wrinkles and the white hair made him the very embodiment of what he had jokingly been called in his youth. Even way back then they had said he'd had an old head on his young shoulders. It was one of the reasons that he'd been chosen. Not that he'd had much of a choice. None of them did.

Well, now his outward appearance reflected exactly how he felt and with age had come acceptance. He chuckled to himself. Acceptance and, occasionally, wisdom. He knew what it was he had to do.

Iain would be fine. He was married. He had a job he enjoyed and a family he loved. Jen... He smiled as he recalled her to mind. All red hair and attitude. Jen would find her way. Eventually. If she didn't get expelled first. He chuckled. Jen would be fine.

Once upon a time he would have felt a thrill at what lay ahead, at what he was about to do, but this morning all he felt was weariness. Weariness and a creeping sense of despair at just how much still needed to be done. Time, at least for him, was running out. So much to do and so little time left to do it.

He sighed. Time. It always came down to time. How he wished he had never started this. Never taken hold of that hand.

He reached out. His fingers tracing over the lines, the circles. He hesitated, taking one last look around... taking in the glen that he had called home most of his life.

He touched the ring, golden light spreading outwards. Taking a deep breath, he braced himself. There was a silent pop. And he was gone.

Circles and Stones

Into the now empty clearing echoed the mournful call of the crow.

Chapter 1

I sighed. The face in the mirror sighed back. Nine weeks of this. Nine weeks without school. Nine weeks of being forced to go on walks and 'appreciate' nature. I didn't need to go on walks to appreciate what was out there. I mean, don't get me wrong, I love the outdoors. I loved camping. I'd been enrolled in the Duke of Edinburgh Awards Scheme with the rest of the kids when we all started High School.

Currently working towards my Silver Award, I might add. Go Team!

As a result, I could build a fire with the best of them and could, if pushed, make a damn fine cup of tea.

Why anyone would drink tea when coffee was an option was beyond me. I mean, really.

It's just that, I guess, when push came to shove, I much preferred it to be on my own terms. Being "forced" to do anything was, well, it just didn't sit well with me. And I mean, c'mon, it's not like Kilmartin Glen was exactly in the wilds. Ok.

Yes. The nearest coffee shop was all the way down in Lochgilphead and the phone signal could barely even be described as 3G but still, you were never more than a couple of hours walk away from the main road and from there you could hitch a lift to anywhere. So long as your parents never found out that is. My dad would go SPARE if he ever found out that I'd done that.

Seriously.

I could quite happily appreciate nature from here. Or from the museum. Especially when you consider that my pale, whiter than white skin and flaming red hair weren't exactly summer sun friendly and that the midges, nasty horrible bitey insects, were so big they carried knives and forks.

That being said, I was at least honest enough to admit that my current predicament was all my own fault. I was still at a loss as to what had possessed me but what's done is done.

It seemed like the moment they had been called up to the school (to be given the news that I was being suspended) Mum and Dad had been a whirlwind of activity and the following morning I was once again bundled into the car and dragged (not exactly kicking and screaming I might add) to the Glen - to granny and 'adads cottage. Anytime there was some sort of crisis or family emergency...

I can't believe I am classing myself as a family emergency.

...we inevitably fled to the Glen. Kilmartin Glen.

Dad and his sister had been born here, in the little whitewashed cottage. Granny had died here and 'adad... Well, after Gran had died, 'adad just kinda became more and more distant until one day he wasn't really there anymore. He just... Vanished.

Now when I say vanished, I don't mean he left, I mean he quite literally vanished. Went out for a walk one morning and just never came back. It caused quite the hoo-ha at the time.

Local man vanishes!!!

There were newspapers and reporters and everything. I think we even made it onto the local radio but, as with all such things, time passes. People find other things to talk about. Eventually even the conspiracy theorists left well enough alone. He was declared missing, presumed dead and everyone just kinda moved on. Everyone just kinda forgot.

Everyone except me.

I mean c'mon. People don't just vanish. At the very least there would have been a body. If he'd fallen or tripped or even drowned.

There would. Have been. A body.

But no. No sign of an accident. No indication of foul play. No body. He was just... Gone.

And everyone seemed to be perfectly fine with that? Seriously? Well. Not me. I wasn't old enough to really understand what was going on with gran, or so I was told, so I don't really remember her being ill. I do remember the fights though, the arguments. 'adad was so angry. I mean I guess I can understand why but... Well, it seemed excessive, even to me. Both of them were gone in a matter of weeks. All my joy in this place faded when they died.

I sighed…

Nine weeks...

Circles and Stones

"You are not going out looking like that!" Jerked to a halt by her words I looked down, unsure of what had precipitated the outburst this time.

"Iain... tell her!" Mum was standing by the table under the window, the worksurface covered in plants. Even from over here I could see Dandelions, Nettles, all the fun stuff you find in the garden. If I didn't get out of here quickly, I had no doubt that I'd be dragooned into going down to the bogs at Dunadd to get some Myrtle. Bog Myrtle that is.

Mum's a botanist. Every year whilst we're in the Glen on holiday she turns her degree into a small money-making exercise. Teas... Candles... Scented oils... You name it, that woman could make it, and most likely make money from it. I'd tried some of her concoctions and truth be told I'm not a huge fan. About the only one I could actually stomach was her Dandelion tea. Good for the digestion apparently. Oh. And the Bog Myrtle. That's the Important one. Especially in this part of the country. She makes this lotion? Perfume? Whatever. It scares off the midges. They hate it. I didn't get on with midges, so it was very much a win win situation from my point of view. Not only that it kept her busy and out of my hair. Or what was left of it.

Dad lifted his head out of whatever it was he was reading and scrutinised me... He gave the slightest shrug and motioned at the door with a flick of his eyes... "I dunno, I think she looks fine..." Needing no more encouragement I grabbed my keys and was out the door and heading down the path before mum's voice went through the roof... She'd been at me ever since I'd come home from school, and she saw what I'd done to my hair. I mean, It's my hair. I have to live with it. I can do what I want. Thus went my reasoning. The fact that I'd been suspended was completely incidental in her mind. That I'd shaved the sides of my head was infinitely worse.

Yeah, I can see what you're thinking, What 15-year-old uses words like thus? Well, I read. A lot. Sue me.

I mean, don't get me wrong, I'd realised it was a mistake almost as soon as the clippers touched my head, but I wasn't going to admit that. Not to my friends and certainly not to my mother. It's not that I was impulsive or anything, I'd thought about getting my head shaved for weeks before I actually did the deed. I figured if I was gonna be known for my hair...

Which was the gingerest ginger you have ever seen by the way. A gift from some unknown and unnamed ancestor, but once it's in your genes, you're pretty much stuck with it.

...Then I may as well be known for something other than its colour. Maybe one day I'd learn.

That was what everyone said. "One of these days Jen, you will learn." Some days I almost believed them. Still, the sun was shining, the birds were singing. It was a beautiful day, and I was gonna make the most of it. The Glen was spread out before me, and the day was mine. I used to love coming here, the long walks. Exploring "fields of stone" as my gran used to say. 'adad and I could lose entire days just walking from hill to moor, from circles to stones. He never seemed to tire and was a wellspring of endless delight. The things that man knew. Every other day he'd tell me that it was so many years since such and such an event. So many years from such and such a person dying. It was funny. He always used to describe things like that. He'd never say, "It's your birthday in 5 days!" Instead, it'd be "Well Jen it's been 360 days since your last birthday."

The tears, surprisingly close to the surface this morning threatened to spill but I resisted the temptation and continued on my course. My feet following the trail we'd walked, over and over, year after year. Up the hill to the ancient rock carvings. It had been three years since he'd left.

Ha! There I go again. Since he left. Mum was forever giving me grief for that, even Dad had eventually frowned at me for saying that.

"He's dead Jen." He'd said. "Dead and gone where you can't follow." It had been fairly brutal but sometimes I get so wrapped up in my own head that I forget that I wasn't the only person who had lost someone. At the top of the hill, I stopped. Just stopped, shut my eyes, and breathed in the silence. It was always so quiet up here… The sounds of birds singing in the trees faded to nothing as I stood. He'd been heading here on the day he'd left. It had never been said, but I knew. I knew he'd been coming here. It's where he came every day. It's where I came every time I was here. It was almost a compulsion. I could feel him here. Sometimes, I even talked to him. Occasionally, I thought he answered.

I know. It's daft. But haven't you ever been somewhere that felt particularly close to someone? As if over the years their continued presence had left an echo? No? Ok. Just me then.

It really was a beautiful day and the peace of the place beckoned me onwards. I climbed the little fence and made my way out onto the expanse of sun-warmed rock. It never ceased to amaze me.

The large expanse of naked stone was cut and carved with circles and whorls and spirals, swirling and twisting, catching the eye, tugging on the soul. It's so easy to just lose yourself in the patterns, to lose track of time. Minutes became hours, hours became days. There were times when I would lie here and just let my mind wander. Hours would take flight. Once I even fell asleep. Mum had sent dad to look for me that day. I swear I'd never seen him so angry. Before or since.

I traced the details of a carving with my finger, marvelling at the skill. It must have taken weeks to make these... Tap tap tapping... I closed my eyes... I could imagine them sitting here, scraping these markings into the stone. Grinding out cup marks, the sun shining down.

I could almost hear them as they carved. Talking, whispering, shouting. Voices echoing out of the past; "Theirig air ais!!* Theirig air ais agus dùsgadh!!* Jen!! Theirig air ais agus dùsgadh!!"

I awoke with a start. The faint whispers of words echoing in my mind. "What on earth?" I looked about, still not grasping where I was, it felt like hours had passed as I lay dreaming on this hill. I glanced at my watch. "Oh my god!! 4.45!!!!" I was sooooo going to get it. Not only had I slept through lunch, but I was now in imminent danger of missing dinner. Mum was going to go spare! I grabbed my stuff and ran for it.

It took me all of 15 minutes to get home, but I was still late. I burst in, apology at the ready but the scene which greeted me was exactly the same as that which I'd left nearly seven hours before... Dad at the table, reading. Mum, chopping plants. "I'm so sorry..." I began. Mum glanced up and sighed, "What have you done this time?"

"I'm late?" Dad looked up; eyebrow raised in askance. "I'm sorry," I rushed on, "I didn't mean to, I just lost track of time. I was up at the circles and the sun was shining and I shut my eyes. I was listening to the voices, and I must have just dozed off. I didn't mean to..."

Dad had turned to look directly at me. "What do you mean you were listening to the voices?" The look on his face made me pause, "I... It must have been walkers or people up to the see the circles, but I could have sworn I could hear someone shouting in Gaelic."

He opened his mouth to say something but was interrupted by mum. "Really Jen you've barely been gone 20 minutes." She paused, staring at me, her eyes narrowing. "At least you could have worn a hat! You're already turning pink!! You hear me?? Wear a hat when you go out! It's the least you could do since you butchered your hair!"

What is it with her obsession with my hair?

"Now scoot! I'm not having you moping about in the house. It's the first day of summer and the last thing I need is you under my feet and getting in my way all day. Out!!" Dad looked at me on my way past and I knew, I just knew we were going to talk about this later. Dad had issues about me falling asleep in public spaces. Personal safety was never really high up on my list of priorities and the way he was frowning at me suggested I'd be getting a talking to at some point today.

The fun never stops in my house, can you tell?

Point made, he broke eye contact and, grabbing a hat on the way, out I went.

******

Some people will claim that it's not actually possible to wander aimlessly but I'm here to tell you that's not true. I mean, if you stop paying attention to where you are going, it's not like you stop moving is it? No. You keep going. It's what I refer to as wandering feet. I am frequently distracted (you may have noticed) and in the event of my attention being on other, more important things, my feet just kinda take charge. It keeps me moving and out of trouble, so I just give them free reign. Today, when I left the cottage, I was most definitely distracted. My watch, my awesome, totally retro, Casio digital watch told me I'd been asleep on the hill for seven hours and yet my eyes (and my mother) claimed that I'd been gone for only 20 minutes. I can understand a wind-up watch losing time, or even my digital one if I'd been exposed to some sort of electromagnetic field...

Hey, can't a girl watch the X Files? The truth is out there people.

...But to actually gain time?? Now, call me old fashioned, but for some reason I kinda doubted I'd been abducted by aliens. Fairies? Yes... I mean the Glen was just overflowing with burial mounds... What was it the Irish called them? Sidhe? That was it. Fairy mounds. The entrance to their Fairy Realm. Ireland was even more crowded with fairy structures than the Glen. Mounds, Hills, Stones, hell, they even had fairy trees! People were reputed to go missing for DAYS although, I quietly attributed that more to the Guinness and the Stag and Hen parties than to any sort of supernatural shenanigans.

I paused and took in my surroundings. Main road. Heading north. My feet obviously knew what they were doing so I left them to it. They seemed pretty determined to head towards the village, as indicated by a convenient signpost "A816 Cille Mhartainn".

That's Kilmartin for those of us who don't understand Gaelic.

Having exhausted all speculation as to whether it had been aliens or fairies who had meddled with my watch, I decided it was time to relieve my feet of the burden of decision making, and headed down into the village, although, strictly speaking, calling it a village was pushing the definition to the very limit. It was, quite literally, a church, a museum, a castle, and a cafe.

Maybe a couple of houses. People gotta live somewhere, right?

Oh, And the most extensive collection of standing stones and rock carvings and tombs to be found anywhere in the country. You could quite literally fall over a monolith (and most likely hurt yourself) in the Glen if you weren't careful. They were everywhere. From my vantage point I could see, without really trying, four cairns, two stone circles, numerous standing stones and a henge to boot. And that's just those that were visible. If you truly wanted to know more about the history of the place, then you needed to speak to Callie down at the museum. For all that she'd only been here a couple of years, this was a woman who knew her cairns from her cists.

The museum was a bit of a haven, a safe space for me. It was dark. It was quiet and it was filled with really cool stuff. It was without a doubt one of my favourite places in the glen. The summer after gran had died and 'adad had left, I'd pretty much been left to my own devices. Dad was devastated and mum, well mum had her hands full dealing with the media and Dad (and her own grief). No one had time for me. I'd been adrift on a sea of self-pity for a couple of weeks and eventually the tides of fortune had cast me ashore here.

That was when I had met Callie. She had only recently arrived but already knew sooo much about the history of this place (and the whole of these Islands truth be told). What had originally been a place of mystery and wonder began to take on new depths as, over the course of the summer, she taught me about the people who had lived here, those shadows from history who had erected the monuments. It didn't lessen the mystery or the wonder, but it sure gave me a whole new appreciation as to what the people of that time period were capable of. We talked for hours, day after day. Myths. Legends. Boggles. Brownies. She even told me a story about weird lights in the sky out by Dunchraigaig. She knew it all, and by the end of that first summer we had become firm friends. If I'm being honest, it was largely thanks to her that I got through that summer at all. It was rough going for a while. Every time I'm in the Glen I still end up spending most of my spare time down in the museum, it was cool, it was quiet and quite frankly unless I had a question that quite simple HAD to be answered right now this minute then Callie pretty much left me to my own devices. I pushed open the door and stuck my head in... "CAAAAALLIE?!?!" No answer. Not unusual, and it's not like I've never visited unannounced before. It wouldn't be the first time she had come into work or back from lunch to find me lying in a corner, face stuck in a book, when things got a bit tense at home.

It looked like they were getting ready for an exhibition. It had all changed since I'd last been here and there were rows upon rows of display cases with things I'd never seen before. Things that had been found in digs all up and down the Glen. Things on loan from the Museum in Edinburgh. This was gonna be a BIG exhibition!!

I heard a door shut in the darkness and a voice rang out "Hello???" Footsteps echoed through the hall and eventually the white-haired head of Callie appeared out of the darkness. Followed by the rest of her I might add. No disembodied heads round here thank you very much.

"Oh..." She blinked at me through the darkness, "I wondered who on earth would be keen enough to be breaking in here at this time of day."

I smiled, "Hey Callie, that's some nice stuff you've got here. Whose arm did you have to twist to get these goodies all the way out here?"

She smiled, "Oh, you know, talk to the right people. In the right time, in the right places... Her voice tailed off and she stared at me before continuing. "A little bird told me you'd been suspended..." I could hear the disapproval in her voice. "What, pray tell, did you do to incur the wrath of the headmaster this year?" I gestured to my hair. "Oh..." She laughed, "Well, I guess I can understand why your mum went a bit mental, but truth be told I've seen worse. Here..." She tossed me a scrunchy...

I kid you not. An honest to goodness scrunchy.

..."Tie it back. I don't need ginger hair all over the new finds thank you very much."

"Oh? New finds? Dare I ask?" I was always up for something new and interesting.

"Well now," she smiled, warming to her subject, "Out the front here it's mostly items which have been recovered in the glen itself, you know the Ri Cruin cairn? Down by the Bullock Shed? There's a couple of pieces which were in the collection down at Poltalloch House, before it burned down, and of course a couple which were loaned to the museum by your grandfather."

The catch in her voice when she mentioned him made me look at her. As a general rule, if at all possible, we avoided talking about him, I'd always thought it was out of respect for my feelings but the tone of her voice when she mentioned him made me think it was something else. Something more. Never one to take a hint I pushed onwards, " 'adad loaned the museum some pieces?" My voice must have betrayed my surprise. Gesturing at the displays, I asked, "Which pieces did he lend you?"

"They aren't on display yet, but I have them through the back preparing them if you want to come have a look-see." She guided me through the stacks and brought me out into the small office near the front of the building. On the workbench lay two items. The first, a narrow pinkish quartz knife, I'd never seen before, but the second? Well, I was more than familiar with that. It was an irregular shaped object about the size of an egg but flattened on both sides and polished to a mirror like finish. The thing which made it eye catching were the beautiful spirals and circles deeply engraved upon it. It was beautiful and looked like it had come straight from the jewellers. Coincidentally (or maybe not) it was identical to the one which I had in my pocket, with my keys hanging from it.

Noticing my look Callie explained, "Sadly that's just a replica of a piece that your grandfather..." she paused, "found. Though, as far as I'm aware, he never revealed the location of where he'd found it or even let the museum have a proper look to try and date it or otherwise place it in its proper context." She picked it up off the desk and ran her fingers over the design. "The closest they ever got was when he allowed them to photograph it in order to create this replica. After he passed, the museum asked your parents if they would be willing to sell the original, but it was nowhere to be found. One must assume that he took it with him when he left." She paused before correcting herself "When he died." Carefully she placed it back on the desk, putting it down next to the blade. "It was a truly astonishing piece. To my knowledge only one other has ever been found and that one was damaged. Before my time." She muttered, almost to herself. "It sounds like he was a remarkable man, I'm just sorry that he was gone by the time I arrived here.

"Can I hold it?" I looked at her and she nodded, It was the mirror image of the one I had but felt, somehow, subtly different. It was the design which had always intrigued me, spirals and circles randomly arranged. You could almost feel your gaze falling into them. In fact, it was actually kinda reminiscent of the tattoo he'd had on his forearm,

I mean, that in itself isn't unusual. I knew someone who had a tattoo of the brooch of Tara on her back. Some people like tattoos, some people don't. I was firmly in the camp of the former and was totally gonna get one when I was old enough. And yes. Mum would definitely go spare. Just something else to add to her list.

"You know, I think you and 'adad would have probably liked each other. He knew more about this place than just about anyone I have ever met. Present company excluded." She smiled at the compliment. I can still remember sitting on his knee when I was wee, tracing the pattern with my finger, round and round, a spiral etched in faded blue ink. Any time I asked why he had it or what it meant he'd shrug and say, "We all do things when we're young that we sometimes regret."

Breaking my reverie, I put down the amulet and reached for the knife. "May I?" I looked at Callie in askance who nodded. Even as I lifted it, I could feel it. I don't know how to describe it. It just felt odd. "What a bizarre thing for him to have" I exclaimed. "For him to have owned something that was soooo, I don't know, intrinsically violent just seems completely out of character." It certainly wasn't something that he had ever talked about or shown anyone (that I knew of) and the oddity of it just rubbed me the wrong way. I tore my gaze away from the offending item and followed her over to the where she was standing at the window. "All my life I never knew him to even raise his voice, let alone lose his temper."

Other than at Gran during those last few months. But even then, I knew that was different.

Callie snorted "Perhaps you don't know him quite as well as you think you do"

"Did." I corrected her. She looked at me for a second, an odd smile playing across her face. "My apologies… Did."

"Well, If you've got nothing better to do today then you're welcome to hang around here but I've got to head up to the dig this afternoon, in fact I'm probably going to be up and down the glen for the rest of the week, why don't you swing by and join us at the dig tomorrow? You'll no doubt be wandering about looking for trouble anyway and at least this way I can keep you from raking about in here and your mum and dad will be pleased that you're actively engaging in doing something productive with your holidays and not wasting time shaving the rest of your head or getting into trouble."

"Are you Serious??? You mean it? You're not just winding me up? I can actually come on a dig???" This was a major development. I mean, I love history, how could I not when you consider where I spent my summers, It was everywhere you turned here. But to actually get in and about it and get my hands dirty as it were? That was a whole different ball game. Just looking at the pretty stones paled in comparison to trying to understand how they were built and swapping speculation with the rest of the students as to why.

Head buzzing with excitement I took my leave, and headed home... This summer might not be a complete loss after all.

Chapter 2

The 20th dawned bright and sunny and thank God it was dry. I'd arrived home the day before to find my dad waiting, lecture already prepared. By the time I went to bed I was fully aware of how irresponsible I was and how dangerous it was falling asleep in public places and how I obviously didn't think of anyone but myself oh and don't forget the extra serving of guilt about not considering how my poor mother would have felt if anything untoward had happened to me. I'd tried to point out there wasn't anyone there and the voices must just have been the tail end of a dream which surprisingly brought his tirade to an abrupt halt.

"What do you mean? That the voices were in your head?" He looked worried, almost scared. Not that I can really blame him. Admitting that you hear voices. Even to your dad, isn't the sort of thing to inspire confidence. I mean, it wasn't like I was hearing voices in my head. They were definitely external. Just... Not really. I wasn't helping myself here and with a final shake of his head he muttered "Dia cuidich mi" and was gone.

It's always nice when my dad mutters at me in Gaelic. Anyway. What was I saying? Oh yes. It was bright and sunny and thank God it was dry. I mean don't get me wrong, spending the day on my hands and knees in a muddy hole sounded about as close to heaven as I was likely to get but doing it whilst it was raining? Or even worse when the smirr came rolling down the sides of the hills into the valley and soaked everything in sight? Now that would not be a pleasant experience.

Suited and booted I headed down the stairs where wonder of wonders I find a packed lunch and a note. "Wear a hat!!!!!"

And yes, that's FIVE (count 'em) exclamation marks.

The house was already empty, so I grabbed my keys, locked up and headed out. The dig, which had been going on intermittently since the previous year was focussed on the stone circles at Temple Wood but there were also small, related digs scattered up and down the glen, added to all that there was a team from one of the universities digitally recording the many cup and ring sites which, even by my limited knowledge, would probably take them the rest of their lives.

Crossing the road I paused, there were two ways I could go here, I could keep following the road, past the bullock shed then turn right. A walk of another couple of hundred yards and I'd be there. Ooooorrrrrr I could jump the wall, cross the fields and head there directly. It was a no brainer really. Crossing the fields, it is.

What? There are standing stones in the field. I never missed an opportunity to admire them up close. Not if I could help it.

Needless to say, in my rush to appreciate some neolithic stonework, I completely forgot that what looks likes dry land hereabouts is most often a lie. A dirty. Filthy. Lie. I hopped over the wall and was forcibly reminded of this by the fact that I sank, almost immediately, right up to my knees in mud. Black. Sticky. Sucking, and above all smelly, mud. Oh, the joys. With difficulty, and almost losing my boot in the process, I extracted myself from the ghastly stuff and clambered back over the wall. Maybe the road wasn't such a bad idea after all, and it did give me the most fabulous, (but more importantly, dry) view of the cairns and standing stones along the way.

Even from this distance I could hear the chatter and the noise of the dig which almost (but not quite) made me forget about the squelching in my boots... It was gonna be such an awesome day.

I turned down the track and there sitting on the wall, watching me approach was Callie. I waved. "I'm sorry I'm late but... Um... I had a wee accident."

"I saw" she laughed, "you know, there's a reason that we use roads and paths and stuff round here yeah??"

"Yeah, yeah" I laughed. I looked around, anxious to be doing something... "So, what's the craic? Where do you want me? Can I have a trowel?"

She laughed. "Slow down Red.!! We'll get there... First let's see if we can't find you some dry boots, If I send you home with trench foot, your mum will most likely have you confined to the house for the rest of the summer. Not to mention making my life a living hell into the bargain."

She had a point, so I followed her over to the main tent. Looking about I noticed there were two or three people I recognised but there were dozens more who I did not. In fact, the place was busier than I had ever seen it. I mean, yes, Kilmartin was blessed with an abundance of ancient things like this, but it was also pretty much in the middle of nowhere. In fact, you had to drive past the middle of nowhere to get here. Probably one of the reasons as to why it was still so untouched by the trappings of civilisation. No Starbucks...

Which was severely testing me by the way. Caffeine withdrawal is real, people.

...No McDonalds, which quite frankly suited me just fine and virtually no phone signal, which really didn't. All that aside, it really had to be said, today was going to be a good day. Just me, Callie, and two ancient stone circles.

Oh. And the twins. Damnit. How I loathed the twins. Nikki and Hillary. They were only a year older than me but to hear them tell it, the gap may as well have been ten. In a village this small you made friends with whoever you could. I'd tried, lord knows I'd tried but they were having none of it. Ach well, it wasn't like I'd be able to avoid them all summer. Believe it or not, my mum gave me the best advice about the twins. "Ignore them and move on." The last thing I wanted, was to get into a screaming match with them and get thrown off the dig or, even worse, disappoint Callie who at that moment handed me a wad of paper and a stick of charcoal and pointed me towards the smaller (and apparently, the older) of the stone circles. I'd only taken a couple of steps when I saw him...

He wasn't exactly hard to miss.

...taller than me but with the same bright red hair. "Ruairidh!" He smiled and waved. "And a good day to you Genevieve."

Not a word! You hear me? Not one word!!

I blushed. I swear he does this to me every time. NO ONE calls me by my Sunday name. I'd bitched and moaned about it so often that even my mum had given up on that one. But Ruairidh could not be dissuaded and so every time we met, I end up standing there with a face even redder than my hair.

Speaking of which, he gestured at my hair, "No tattoos... No piercings... I have to admit that I'm a bit disappointed. For someone who is supposed to have shaved their head and joined a cult you're looking suspiciously normal."

OMG! Had my mum told everyone?

Ignoring the invitation to banter I looked about. "Where do you want me? Callie said you were the man with the plan."

"I am indeed the man, with the plan. This morning I need you to get in amongst the uprights over there and find the petroglyphs. Callie wants a decent rubbing of them for the exhibition." My face fell. "Or, if you'd rather, you can help the twins dig a new waste pit for the latrine."

"No, no, Its fine." I assured him quickly. Possibly too quickly. I'm not sure what would be worse. Digging a new poop hole. Or working with the twins. I shuddered. "A rubbing, was it?"

He smiled, "This is important too, and if you make a habit of joining us then your gonna have all summer to get your hands dirty." He leant forward to whisper, "And it'll keep you away from the twins, so, happy days yeah?"

Reluctantly, I accepted my charge and trudged back the way I had come, Ruairidh shouted at my retreating back, "See if you have better luck than Nikki, she searched for HOURS yesterday and came up with nothing."

Great. Now it was a competition. This was never gonna end well. These things never do.

OK... a brief description is probably in order about now. The Glen. At the northern end is the Village. Kilmartin. At the south... the ancient hillfort of Dunadd. Running between the two and right down the middle of the glen is a linear cemetery - a series of burial cairns. Rows of standing stones. Stone circles. Solitary monoliths and petroglyphs. Almost everywhere you looked. Petroglyphs. It seemed that every exposed rock surface was covered in them. It was an archaeologists playground and this summer, they had all come out to play.

Temple Wood... Goodness, where to begin? The big circle was less a circle and more a kind of horseshoe pattern with the opening to the south-east. Small cobble like stones fill the centre, looking remarkably similar to pictures of cairns I'd seen up near Inverness. Within the circumference of the stones were two cist graves. Once upon a time it had been a complete circle but some of the stones had been removed, no doubt ending up as part of someone's house or in any one of the multitude of walls hereabouts. I figure I'd just start at one end and work my way round. I am in no doubt that Callie or Ruairidh could tell me exactly which stones had the carvings on them but where would the fun be in that.

As the sun inched its way across the sky the temperature started to rise, don't get me wrong, we're in Scotland so it's not like there was any real danger of the us losing that pale blue tinge to our complexion but, as anyone similarly afflicted can tell you, ginger hair and bright sunshine isn't exactly a good combination, but, shock horror, I wasn't paying the slightest bit of attention to the weather. There were more important things going on. I'd found my first petroglyph!!

Yes, I know it's been found and catalogued many many times before but the thrill of finding something like this. It was like Christmas and Easter and all my birthdays rolled into one. It was beautiful. Don't get me wrong, it was of an incredibly simple design, nothing at all like the large panels of rock art to be found elsewhere in the glen but that was irrelevant. I'd never seen it before, so for just that moment in time, it felt like it was all mine. Two concentric rings carved on the stone at the very northern edge of the circle. Very faint. Almost a blink and you'd miss it, but it was definitely there!!! I'd found it!! I could see Callie grinning at my reaction and in the sheer joy of discovery I completely missed the glares from behind me.

One rubbing in the bag I moved on. There weren't that many stones left, surely the second carving was here somewhere. I was sitting running my fingers over the surface of the stone in front of me trying to discern any change in texture on the surface when something caught my eye. The stones were all a uniform grey. I mean, if you looked up grey in the dictionary, there would probably be a picture of one of these stones. But there, on the next one along, was a glittering nodule of quartz wedged into what, for want of a better word, looked like a keyhole. Every time I changed position it glittered in the sun. Temporarily I abandoned my search for stone carvings and approached the shiny. I poked it with my stick of charcoal. It wobbled.

Now, the first rule of Archaeology club is: You don't talk about archaeology club.

I mean it. Have you ever tried to maintain your social standing if anyone finds out you like to spend your time digging holes in the ground??

The second rule is: DON'T TOUCH ANYTHING!!! Mindful of this I wave at Callie. She wandered over, "Sup??" I pointed down at the stone. "Oh well done!! You've found the second carving." Puzzled, I looked down and sure enough at the base, radiating out from the "keyhole" was a magnificent spiral...

A magnificent spiral that looked suspiciously like the one on my keyring (which was currently burning a hole in pocket.) In fact, it looked exactly like it.

She started to move off, "Callie, that's not what I wanted to show you. It's that. There, can you see??" I pointed at the quartz with my charcoal...

She got down on her knees and stared at it. Eventually she muttered something in what sounded like exasperation. "It's probably just been wedged in there by some tourists." She handed me her trowel, "See if you can't pop it out for me."

I took the trowel and gently slid it into the hole and tried to pop the stone out... It was quite loose and with a final wiggle it slid out into my hand. What I'd originally thought to be just a shiny quartz pebble lodged in a small hole turned out to be shaped like a long crystal blade. A pale milky pink in colour. Surprised I nearly dropped it. I made a grab for it and, the moment my fingers wrapped round it, I knew I'd made a mistake.

Gosh. Did it suddenly get hot??? Suddenly I was feeling light-headed. I glanced down at what I had in my hand, the trowel, suddenly too heavy to hold, fell from my grasp. I tried to stand up. Why wouldn't the ground just stay still?! Deciding that being closer to the ground was infinitely safer I dropped to my knees. "CALLIE!!! "CAAAAAAAALLIE!!"

I could almost hear her sigh. But then she was there. "Dear god Jen where is your hat????"

I couldn't even lift my head to look at her. "Could you just get me something to drink?? I'm desperately trying not to throw up here..."

Circles and Stones

As I knelt there, I could feel it. It was almost as though my hand were wrapped around a live wire. I couldn't let go. Another pulse and my grip on the thing tightened. I could feel it cutting into my hand. Another spasm and blood was welling up between my fingers... Callie was fussing. Calling for water. Saying something about sunstroke... "CALLIE!!! LOOK!!!"

She turned, her eyes following mine down to my hand, "Oh my god Jen! What have you done? Your hand!! You're bleeding!! Her eyes widened. She looked about, almost in a panic I thought. "You're BLEEDING!!! Hilary!!! get me a plastic bag!! NOW!!!!" She's staring me in the eyes. "Hold your hand up Jen, up above your head, It will slow the bleeding. DO NOT UNDER ANY CIRCUMSTANCES OPEN YOUR HAND!! So help me god if you let your blood contaminate this site!!"

I just wanted to let go, to lie down. The buzzing in my ears again, louder this time.

Finally, Hilary arrived. "Ok Jen, just put your hand into the bag, That's right." The bag went all the way up to my elbow which, to my addled brain, seemed a bit excessive, "Ok, you can let go now. Let go of the knife..."

Hilary snorted, "Amadan ruadh!"

I whipped round towards her, suddenly, irrationally, furious. "Callie bhan!! Radh a-rithist!!"

"Enough!!" Callie interrupted the fight before it could get started. "Jesus, Hilary this isn't the time!! Jen, come with me!!"

She led me away towards the site office (see: tent) Once inside I dropped to my knees and was noisily (and embarrassingly) sick. God, I was never going to live this down. The whole dig would know. Then the village. Then my mum. This was not the start to the summer that I'd anticipated.

Callie let go of my hair and crouched down opposite me, handing me a big bottle of water. I gratefully washed out my mouth and drank. She grinned, "Better?" I nodded. "Next time you might want to think about wearing a hat. I know, I know. I probably sound like your mother, but you might want to give her a break. She isn't wrong as often as you'd like to think." I had the grace to at least acknowledge her point.

"But I brought a hat!! I was wearing a hat." I looked about. "It must have fallen off when I was doing my first rubbing. I have no idea where it is." I pressed my hand to my forehead and closed my eyes, God my head hurt. This was shaping up to be the mother of all headaches. I struggled to stand up.

Damnit, this ground just wasn't up for staying still, was it? Callie gently pushed me back down "Stay there for a while. Its ok." She smiled, "You never told me you were learning Gaelic at school. I thought you were of the opinion that it was a dying language and it should be left to die in peace?"

"I... I'm not learning it. Why on earth would I want to learn Gaelic?" She frowned at me, "I'm Serious. I don't speak it." I wasn't trying to be funny, I know how interested Callie is in the ancient Celts and that includes their languages. I'm pretty sure she could also speak Welsh, possibly even Manx but I just couldn't see the point. That being said, I wasn't about to mock someone who did.

"Jen... You're speaking it right now. We've been speaking in Gaelic since we left the circles. Since you called Hilary a blonde hag."

Ok... A joke's a joke but can we just stop now?? I'm slowly bleeding to death here. I struggled to stand up again and biology finally did what gravity had been trying to encourage for the last 20 minutes and I fainted.

I came too to the sound of swearing. "Jen!!! Oh my god you gave me such a fright. Are you ok? How do you feel? Here, drink this water."

Everything seemed to be back to working within normal parameters. Even my hand had stopped throbbing.

"Have you any idea what you've found Jen?" I mean, its broken and it's missing its handle but it's virtually identical to the one that Gwyn loaned the museum before he left!!

The blank look must have betrayed my confusion. "Your granddad, Jen…"

I tried to shake my head, but it still felt that any sudden movement might dislodge it entirely, "That wasn't his name, his name was Malcolm."

She laughed incredulously. "Malcolm?" She laughed again. "I knew him for a lot longer than you so if its ok then I think I'll be sticking with Gwyn."

"How can that be??? How could you have known 'adad? He was gone before you ever came here! When did you find the time to get to know him at all?" I think I might have stepped over a line cause the look on her face changed. She became all business. Callie the friend, replaced by Callie the adult.

"I think I'm going to need to take you home Jen. Don't worry," she reassured me, "I'm not annoyed but look at you, your hand is probably going to need stitches, God knows what your mums going to say and, quite frankly, you've probably got sunstroke. C'mon, get your things. It might be best if you stay away tomorrow." She must have noticed the expression on my face because she backtracked a little. "Well... You could always come with me up to Achnabreac to check on the students who are doing the recording. Just a quick walk up the hill. It'll give us a chance to talk. I can let you know if I find anything interesting on preliminary studies of that blade you found." She looked at me and nodded, as if coming to a decision,

I nodded in agreement. "That would be great, you can tell me more about how it is that you knew 'adad." She flinched as if I had slapped her. "I mean, if that's ok" I added belatedly.

And so ended my first ever archaeological dig. Six stitches in my hand. Two stone rubbings and a quartz knife. Not a bad haul if I don't say so myself.

Go me! I didn't remember about the whole Gaelic thing till later. Much, much later, and by then it was way too late to ask anyone.

Chapter 3

I was awoken by my alarm the following morning. Callie had said to meet her in the car park at 9am sharp and after yesterday's debacle I really didn't want to be late, I even debated getting dad to give me a lift but by the sound of it everyone was still in bed, so I packed a lunch, grabbed my keys and a hat...

Seriously... I may be stubborn but I'm not a complete idiot.

I locked the door behind me and headed out. Looking up at the sky, it promised to be another gorgeous day.

The circles, as I call them, are actually what most official type people call petroglyphs. Rock cut pictures. They come in many different shapes and sizes, from the massive pictures of horses cut into the chalk downs of England to simple little dimples ground into standing stones. Here in the Glen, the majority of petroglyphs to be found are mainly of the cup and ring variety. Off the top of my head, I could think of, at the very least, five large collections within hiking distance of my house. There was Baluachraig, literally across the road (where I was heading to meet Callie). Ormaig further to the north. Achnabreac and Cairnbaan to the south and Kilmichael in the next glen over. I loved them all. There was just something about them. Weird things had a habit of happening. Things would go missing and turn up days later. Time had a habit of speeding up or slowing down, though, maybe that was just me. Quite often there would be a tangible drop in temperature. You could feel it, but it wouldn't register on any sort of instrument. Like I said. Weird things.

She was already waiting for me when I arrived. I began to apologise but she waved it away. "I was already up at Baluachraig checking things over, but everything seems to be ok. They're gonna finish up here and then head down to meet us at Achnabreac later on." She opened the door of her battered Land Rover, "Jump in."

We drove in silence. And not the comfortable kind. Something had changed since yesterday. Eventually, unable to cope with it, I cleared my throat... "Uh, about yesterday."

She looked at me sideways. "Yes, about yesterday... I don't mind telling you that you gave me quite the scare. All sorts of things could have happened if you'd spilt blood within the stones"

"Oh god I hope I didn't contaminate anything! The Blade?? Could you still date it even though it was covered in my blood??"

"Oh, don't worry about that," she replied, laughing, I know exactly where and when that blade came from."

I heaved a sigh of relief. "Thank goodness, I was worried that I'd completely ruined it.

Circles and Stones

"Its fine," she replied, never taking her eyes from the road, "No harm, no foul." We reached the turn off and pulled into the carpark. Well, actually more of a clearing, just off the road, with a forestry path heading up the hill, leading into the woods. In the shade of the trees, a chill had descended, and goose bumps rose on my arms.

As we started walking something occurred to me. I turned and looked at Callie. Her silence was becoming more than a bit awkward, and I felt the need to fill it. "Don't you think it's odd though??? I mean, the blade was almost exactly the same as the one which 'adad loaned the museum. It was stuck in the rock right next to a carving, which was identical to the engraving on the amulet, which was itself the same as his tattoo."

She laughed. "His Tattoo???" You mean like this one?? She stretched out her arm and there on the inside of her wrist, broken and disfigured by a scar that ran right up to the elbow was a faded blue tattoo... My confusion must have been writ large on my face because she smiled before continuing. "Your granddad and I go way back. We were friends once. Back when we were young. We were chosen on the same day, for our... Apprenticeships. I mean. Well... Kind of. It's complicated."

"But how is that possible? Grandad had to be almost 70! You... Why, you can't be any older than what? 25? 30?"

"27 thank you very much. And I intend on staying that age for the foreseeable future." I laughed, but she looked quite serious. "You see Jen, once upon a time your granddad and I had the same goals, the same dreams. We were friends. More than friends and then, in the midst of everything it all changed. He changed. He did the one thing we were absolutely forbidden to do. The one thing that changed everything. He fell in love. But I fixed that. I fixed her." She spat on the ground as she said it and stalked off, god, she looked angry.

I started after her. "What are you saying? What did you do to my gran?"

She whirled on me "Not your grandmother!!" she snarled. "Do you seriously think your grandfather didn't have a life before he met your grandmother? Before he came here?" She was on a roll now, talking to herself as much as to me. "He had a life before you. Before your father. He had a life!!"

She turned, facing me, staring at me. I took a step back. "I knew him better than you ever will. Better than you ever could. And I know exactly what he is capable of." She glared at me. "And then you had to come home. You had to get suspended and come home early. You are so like him Jen. Painfully so... A look... A word... Even the way you walk. You're like an echo of him reaching out from the past to stop me, but it's not going to happen. Not this time. Not again. You'd have learned to use them eventually, how could you not? Hell, you've been using them without even realising what you've been doing... How else do you think you learned Gaelic? Didn't it strike you as odd? Falling asleep on a hill and all of a sudden being able to speak and understand a completely different language? You'd have figured it all out eventually. Gwyn was always too smart for his own good as well."

"Callie... What are you talking about?" She was starting to scare me. Her eyes were wide, and she was literally ranting. My hands fumbled in my pockets searching for my keys. It was the only thing I had. The only thing with any weight to it that I could conceivably use to defend myself if she attacked me (as was seeming more and more likely).

She stopped and looked at me, her eyes almost pleading, as if two personalities warred behind her eyes. "I don't want to hurt you Jen, I mean, you're practically one of us. I can see it in you, the potential." She shook her head, as though trying to clear it. "No... He betrayed me once. Never again. I can't allow you to stop me, any more than I would have allowed him. You're already too close to understanding. I just can't risk it..."

She bent down and ran her fingers round one of the circles etched into the stone, clearing it of dirt... Then another... And another... A cup mark here... There... The double circles...

"Callie... I don't know what it is you think that I've done but we can sort it out. We can talk about it"

I pulled out my keys... Trying to look nonchalant but she noticed, her eyes widened. "You have the amulet!! You had it all this time!!" She laughed and this time almost sounded excited. "Oh, this makes everything sooooo much easier." She glanced away, looking down, searching for something. She bent and the moment she was distracted, fingers sweeping over the largest of the circles, I took my chance.

I rushed her.

There was a silent pop.

******

Oh god... I was gonna be sick. What had she done to me? I felt like I had just bungee jumped off the Scott Monument and my stomach still hadn't caught up.

Ok Jen, first things first. Open your eyes.

Darkness. I opened them again. And again. Complete. Darkness. I was starting to panic. Even I, with my casual disregard for personal safety, couldn't contemplate going blind without just a wee bit of panic gnawing at my soul.

Deep breaths. In. And out... Deep, calming, breaths. I turned my head. Left, then right... Trying to find something, anything for my eyes to latch on to. There should be trees, there should be blue skies. Hell, there should be Callie!!! There was nothing. Everything had been swallowed by the darkness. It was absolute.

No wait... Not everything. Was that a light?? There. To my right... Away in the distance, dancing the colour of flame. It was!! It was most definitely a light. I could almost cry with the relief that I felt.

But... That would mean it was night!! IT WAS NIGHT!!! What had she done to me??? Had she hit me with some kind of taser?? I musta been out for HOURS.

Oh god mum was gonna KILL me!!

Ok... I guess it's just a sit and wait scenario. It's fine. Really. It's not the first time I've been away overnight, and let's be honest, walking down a hill, even one as gentle as this one, was a sure-fire way of ending up with a free ride in a helicopter to Oban. With a broken leg. Yeah. Waiting was sounding more and more like the plan of the century.

******

I was absolutely freezing by the time the sun started painting the clouds in pastel shades of pink. About an hour ago nature decided to make my night even better by giving me a first-hand experience of that famous scotch mist.

Circles and Stones

Thick. Cold. And very, very, wet. I wasn't quite soaked to the skin, but it was close. At last, the light began to add definition to my surroundings. It really was a beautiful vista. I could see all the way across the Moine Mhor, those massive boglands that stretch from Dunadd down to the sea by the ferry. I could see the Islands starting to appear: Scarba and hints of Jura teasing out beyond the forests behind Crinan. Something that had been nagging at my mind, desperately trying to get my attention suddenly stopped being subtle and slapped me in the face. Trees Jen!!!! Where are all the trees???

Where are all the trees?! Oh god. Oh god oh god oh god! I shouldn't be able to see anything from up here except a wall of trees. Thanks to the forestry commission I should literally be surrounded by a wall of tall (boring) pine trees.

Something was terribly, terribly wrong. A whole forest of mature trees don't just disappear. It just doesn't happen. Not even in this part of the world!! It's not even as if the ground had been ripped up or anything. It was as if they had never been here. Never been planted.

Ok... Breathe Jen. Calm down. There is bound to be a logical explanation

Yeah right!

I'm not gonna solve anything sitting on top of a hill having a meltdown. I can walk and melt at the same time. At least then I might warm up enough to stop shaking.

Yeah, cause that's totally why I'm shaking.

Turns out that whatever had taken the trees had done a proper thorough job and had taken the road as well. Did I mention that something was wrong? I did? Good. 'Cause I'd hate for you to think I'm taking this nice and calmly because I'm really not. Really really not.

The almost complete silence was starting to get to me. There should be cows mooing, there should be wind in the trees, there should be the sound of cars, but there was nothing. Just a large black crow scolding me from atop the boulders over by. I was crying. I'll admit it. Tears were streaming uncontrollably down my face. Can you blame me?? Seriously. You try it: Get attacked by your friend. Wake up in a world that is familiar, but completely, utterly, incontrovertibly different. Changed. You try all that and then tell me you're not feeling just the teensiest bit emotional.

The road down through what had once been forest had been replaced by a path. Not well worn but definitely a path and what does that mean? That's right, you guessed it. A path suggests people.

Mibbee the zombie apocalypse hadn't occurred whilst I'd been out, after all.

Feeling just that little bit more positive I quickened my pace. Beside me, the crow flew from vantage point to vantage point, its mocking call spurring me on. I tried to remember whether it had been crows or ravens that were sacred to Odin. Ravens. It's gotta be ravens. A god like Odin wouldn't be seen dead with a bird as annoying as a crow.

I trudged on. Answers were at the bottom of the hill somewhere and I was out to get them. That, and the fact that I wasn't entirely convinced that Callie wasn't still out there, somewhere. I'd never seen anyone quite that angry and I wasn't exactly champing at the bit to see it again. As far as I was concerned, a little bit of distance between myself and the curator could only be a good thing.

Circles and Stones

OK. So... Funny thing. You know how I said the road was gone? Well, the road WAS gone. The road through the (missing) woods was gone. The road out of the woods was gone and excuse me for stretching it, I'm pretty sure that judging by the absolute lack of any traffic, that the road to Kilmartin was gone as well. It was as if someone had reached out and hit the reset button. Strangely, this idea seemed to calm me down. I know, I'm grasping at straws here, but it was an explanation. It was a really crappy explanation, but it was all that I had at the moment, and I was gonna ride it for all I was worth.

Without any real plan or any real destination, I found that my feet had taken charge of the situation had struck out towards home.

Down on the valley floor things were not much better, but if I focussed on the familiar, the landscape, the river, the hills then I could forget about the lack of a road. Or traffic. Or trees. What the hell had happened to all the trees?!

Nope. Just stay focussed Jen. Landscape. Rivers. Hills. Landscape. Rivers. Hills. See. Its fine. I can totally do this.

Landscape. Rivers. Hills. A tiny little bit of the calm which had completely deserted me started to creep back into my mind.

Landscape. Rivers. Hills... And stones. Standing stones.

I'd stopped moving. I looked up, taking in where I was and glory of glories, there in front of me stood a stone. Actually, two stones, but the stone that held my attention was huge. At least 12 feet high. The only stone of that size in this area was Dunamuck. These must be the Dunamuck stones! You have no idea the relief I felt.

They were still here.

They were familiar.

They were all shiny and new.

Um... What now?

They were quite literally shiny.

And new.

Did I mention new? Like proper new?

I could feel my already tenuous grip on my emotions starting to crumble. These things coulda been put up yesterday. I could still see the tool marks on them! This just wasn't possible.

An explanation was beginning to form in my mind but even my subconscious took one look at it and slammed the door in its face.

It. Wasn't. Possible!

Ok. I'm fully aware that I'm repeating myself, but what you need to understand is, that to all appearances, I have travelled in time. 5000 years, give or take a millennium or so, (Judging by the appearance of the stone). Now, I don't know where, or even when you are reading this account, but In Scotland, In the 21st Century, that was still pretty much impossible.

I looked about... There should be another pair of stones, just to the north, recumbent...

That's lying down to you and me.

Circles and Stones

…and there they were. Standing upright.

Proud and upright.

Defying me with their very uprightyness.

It was true!! Oh, my giddy aunt it was true. I was in the past!! I was in the (this bit has been censored) past!! Everything just came crashing down at that point.

Chapter 4

There's only so long that you can sit in place and cry. Eventually you just gotta get up and start moving again. The fact that the stones were even here was a comfort. Why? What do you mean why? The stones!! The stones mean there MUST be SOMEONE here, I mean, they don't erect themselves...

At least, I hoped not. That would just be a bit much to believe, even for me.

Seriously Jen?? You're BACK IN TIME!!!!! Nothing about this is normal!!

Ok... Ok... Let's just keep calm. If I AM back in time, then it stands to reason that there must be a way back. I mean forward.

You know what I mean!! Stop Laughing!! This isn't the time for humour!!! Time travel! Even just saying it. TIME TRAVEL!!! I can't believe I'm seriously contemplating this. I mean, c'mon. Time. Travel. Travelling in time!!! HOW???

Or, more importantly... When???? Obviously back, thank god. What? You mean the thought of travelling forward in time and being the only person there doesn't just scream apocalypse at you?

God, what I wouldn't do for a coffee right now. Finally, my caffeine deprived brain arrived at the same conclusion as my feet and I began trudging along what would be, in like a million years, the main road from Kilmartin down to Lochgilphead, until of course, we were confronted by the river.

Sigh

I mean, don't get me wrong, it wasn't deep and it's not exactly fast flowing and you're lucky if its 20 feet wide but c'mon. I was just starting to dry out. I'd gone from focussed to frustrated in the blink of an eye, I think it's safe to say that my emotions were all over the place today but let's try and hold onto this positive 'go get 'em' attitude for a little while longer.

At least until lunch time... Food. There was a thought. Do I still have that Twix in my pocket? Success!!! The day is saved. Some chocolate and caramel, some nice crunchy biscuit, and the day is saved... The crow eyed me greedily from the branch of a tree.

C'mon Jen, its unlikely to be the same one.

I tossed some of my Twix in its direction and it fluttered down to investigate. "You're ok to eat chocolate yeah?"

Cause talking to birds is totally normal. Uh Huh.

After finally managing to convince my new BFF that I had no more to give I stuffed the wrappings back in my pocket.

C'mon... I'm 5000 years in the past, in a pristine world, do you really think I'm gonna start littering?

Newly wet and shivering from the cold I shoved my hands in my pockets and immediately pulled them back out when I jammed my fingers against something. Something hard. Something surprisingly warm, something which in my brief moment of panic I had forgotten.

It was brief!!!

I pulled out my keys. They sat there in my hand. What on earth was it about this thing that had caused Callie to change so dramatically?? I mean, it was just a piece of rock!! I turned to put my back to the sun, and I almost dropped it. It just moved. I swear to God the thing physically moved in my hand. My fingers closed instinctively around it. It was vibrating!! Slowly, finger by finger I opened my hand... There was a warmth radiating from it. It had NEVER done this before. It had never done anything weird at all.

Well... Apart from the unfortunate ability to wear through the lining of your pocket faster than you can say needle and thread.

I'd never really looked at it before. I mean, PROPER looked - it was just a key ring, but it HAD been given to me by 'adad, and Callie did kinda go mental when she saw it so I'm guessing there must be SOMETHING special about it.

It was flat, the size and shape of an egg. Kinda rough and unfinished round the edges but highly polished front and back. It looked like someone had taken a slice of rock and polished both sides... Like those fancy do-da's you see in souvenir shops all over the Highlands, beautiful slices of agate to be used, I dunno, as coasters or something, I guess.

But this felt like metal, not stone and was polished to a mirror like finish and deeply engraved on the surface was golden spiral. What was it about that damn spiral?

'adad had a tattoo exactly the same. Come to think of it, so did Callie. I stood up. Suddenly angry. The urge to throw the stupid thing into the river was almost overwhelming. With difficulty I resisted the urge. Anger is good. Anger keeps you moving. Anger in the right situations will keep you alive.

It also leads you to making some truly monumentally stupid decisions but why ruin a good motivational monologue.

I turned to look at the way I had come. I could see the path stretching back to the hill, I hadn't come nearly as far as I thought, and the sun was climbing the sky towards midday... I really gotta get a move on, it was a good couple of hours walk down to the village.

Correction. Where the village should be.

I turned back, putting the river behind me, and started walking.

The village.

The farther I walked, the more it was starting to dawn on me that there was a very real probability, actually more like a certainty that there would be no village. My walking up the valley was nothing more than an exercise to try and find the source of the light I had seen last night. A flame dancing in the darkness. Fire, even way back then. I mean now... Means three things. It means people. It means heat. Aaaand there is a fairly good chance that it means food.

See?? I hadn't gone completely to pieces. Whilst my feet had been doing all the hard work my mind had kinda rebooted. I came round the spur of the hill and the view opened up before me... Stretching out along the valley floor was the landscape I knew. Cairns... Stones... And over there, Temple Wood. Where all this weirdness began. With smoke rising from it. And was that a tent?

******

It was odd walking down the valley without having to climb over walls. It was just a large meadow now with cairns rising above the buttercups. There were clumps of trees now where before there had been only farmers' fields and in between the trees the yellow flowers moved and swayed like water on golden sea. The weirdness of the morning was compounded as I walked past where Callie had picked me up 12 hours and goodness knows how many thousands of years ago. Even more so as I walked past the spot where my house would stand. I didn't feel the panic working back up into my chest, honest, but I may have picked up my pace, ever so slightly. I had the powerful need to talk to someone. Fingers crossed that, whoever the owner of the tent was, they would have the answers which I so desperately needed. I resolutely ignored the suspiciously new looking Nether Largie Standing stones and kept heading towards Temple Wood...

Oh god was that bacon I could smell?? I almost broke into a run at that point, but caution (finally) prevailed. God alone knew who, or even what, I would find.

I must have been staring into what looked like a campsite for maybe 20 minutes before screwing myself up to the point where I couldn't stand it anymore. I took one last look about and, guided by my nose and my grumbling stomach as much by my curiosity I ventured into the camp. It looked deserted. There was no one tending the fire and the tent appeared to be empty. There was literally no one here.

Seriously people, countryside code 101. No untended fires!!

A voice broke the silence. "Well, it's about time!" I spun round, mouth hanging open in shock. There, sitting with his back to a tree was a man. An old man. Well, not old as such, but not young either. Actually, he felt more than looked old. Don't get me wrong, he didn't look any older than my dad, but every vibe I was getting from him screamed of an age that just didn't match the evidence of my eyes. Don't worry. You'll get what I mean.

"So that was you being inserted last night? I wondered how long it'd take you to make your way down here." The silence between us grew as I desperately tried to remember how to talk. "You're not exactly bending my ear here, I'd have assumed there would be questions, maybe an accusation or two. Possibly even an exclamation. No?" I just stood there, suddenly mute. Stunned into silence. Which, I'm sure you all realise by now is a pretty rare occurrence. He stood and limped over, "How about I start then. My name is" he paused, suddenly wary, "actually, my name isn't really that important. What IS important is that... Sorry. Am I boring you?"

He's talking but I've suddenly become the poster girl of inattention. I'm nodding, I'm even occasionally hearing the odd word but all I can think of is bacon. I swear my mouth was actually watering. "Uh.... Do you mind if I join you for lunch?"

Presumptuous? Me? Not at all.

He blinked owlishly then actually laughed. "Of course." He gestured to the ground. "Sit." I dropped to the ground as if my legs had been cut from beneath me. With a bit more dignity he sat down across from me. "I surreptitiously checked him out whilst he was occupied with the fire, He was slight, almost willowy. Not tall but taller than me. Truth be told he looked like he could do with a decent meal himself, but he wasn't skinny, and given that he was sitting here all by his lonesome, in the wilderness, I had to concede that he probably knew how to look after himself way better than me. He had reddish brown hair with the red turning more to grey. Well, more kinda silver really and the shadow of a beard like he hadn't yet shaved. With all of that going on he still didn't feel any older that what? 30? 35 tops. I surveyed the clearing, planning possible escape routes - not that I had any idea where I could escape to, or if there was even anyone else in the valley who could help me should my dinner date with this mysterious camper turn out to be one of my many, many bad decisions. He was quite literally the only person I had seen since regaining consciousness on the hilltop last night.

"You're looking pretty lost." His voice pulled me back to the issue currently at hand. "I presume you didn't really intend on coming this far back. The dislocation, I've heard, can be quite distressing"

I started... HE KNEW!! Here I was sitting, about to have lunch, with a man who had ANSWERS!! I opened my mouth to ask a relevant, at least semi-intelligent question about my current situation and managed...

"OhmygodhowdidIgethereIhavenoideawhatthehellisgoing onImeanliterallyacoupleofhoursagoIwas..."

Nice Jen. Reeeal smooth.

After I had finally exhausted my vocabulary and paused to take a breath, he sighed. "OK. Let me see if I've got this right. You were thrown back in time. You don't know when in time this is. You've no idea how it happened or how to get back. Is that about, right?" I nodded.

Oh yeah, check me with the info dump.

Circles and Stones

He stood, angrily. If anyone can be said to stand angrily, I'd say he pretty much nailed it. "Blessed Belenos when will they learn!!" He looked down at me, "I think I need to know a little bit more about you and where you came from and how, well, how you came to be here."

"Um... Can I ask when here actually is??"

He grunted, "That's more difficult to answer than you might think. Given that I have no idea as to when you have come from it's kinda hard for me to pinpoint when, from your perspective, this actually is, but if you will bear with me, we shall see if we can't fix that right now."

He came 'round the fire toward me. "Don't worry, I mean you no harm, but this may feel a bit... Odd"

OK. I can literally hear what you're thinking but seriously, it's not like I was overburdened by options here was it? Sometimes you just gotta go with your gut.

He reached out his finger and pressed it to my forehead. Right between the eyes it was. Images started flashing through my mind... Arriving at the camp, trudging down here... The circles, Callie, Mum, Dad, 'adad, getting kicked out of school. Faster and faster... My whole life rewinding, unravelling before my eyes. I could feel myself screaming, faster and faster, my mind spinning out of control then... Nothing.

Jen? Jen! I could feel his hand on my shoulder. I was still sitting up right. It was still daylight. There was still bacon.

Thank god. If I'd gone through this whole blasted magic show only to discover that the bacon was gone then there was gonna be some serious trouble.

He was sitting opposite me... My keyring was in his hand. "Ok. Now this may come as a bit of a shock to you, but you have travelled in time. Travelled quite some distance in time I may add. From your perspective we are currently having lunch 1934 years before the birth of your Christ. The woman who so casually dropped you into this mess is known to me, as is her companion. I'm pretty confident that her intentions were... Well, let's just say she certainly didn't have your best interests at heart and leave it that. On the bright side, she most definitely didn't intend for you to meet me. This time I think she may have made a mistake that was beyond even her ability to predict."

"Wait... What...? You KNOW Callie??" To say I was gobsmacked was an understatement.

"Not KNOW her as such more know OF her. She and her partner have been involved in trying to disrupt the natural order of things for many years now. It's an annoyance more than anything and is ultimately futile. There have been a number of occasions when I have been obliged to step in and advise them to stop or to fix what little damage they have done. I've tried to make her understand that time and nature happens as it must, a stone thrown into the river won't divert the flow, it just causes some ripples and sinks without a trace. Time moves on as it must. But my efforts have been mostly in vain. Bear this in mind on your travels Genevieve, nothing you do can alter what must happen. Small details yes, but the bigger picture remains immutable.

"Oh, thank god! You can send me home??" The morning was definitely taking a turn for the better. First there was the bacon and now this guy could send me home.

"Well now. Therein lies the question. I could, if I were so minded, but I think in this instance, instead of sending you where you want to go, I'm going to have to send you where you NEED to go."

That sound you just heard was my bubble bursting.

"Wait... I'm not sure you understand. I NEED to go home. Mum. Dad. They'll be worried. I've been gone for like a day already, they don't need ANOTHER family member to just disappear... The only place you are sending me is home. Home is where I NEED to be."

He sighed. "You need to understand Jen that from your parents point of view you have, to all intents and purposes, just walked out your front door. I'm not gonna get into a discussion about how time works but when you DO return, I can re-insert you into your own timeline at almost the exact moment that you left it. No one, least of all your parents, will be any the wiser as to whether you've been away for days, weeks, months or even years. From their point of view, you will have been gone for all of five minutes. Take some time and think about it, there is nothing that can be done until the morrow anyway. Until then feel free to explore the valley. There is no one here but myself and I have many things which require my attention before I can turn to the matter of what to do with you."

And with that he walked off. Turns out those much-needed answers were just more questions in disguise which, as I'm sure you're aware, is frustrating beyond belief. Damn it. I had this wild urge to just storm off which, let's be honest, wouldn't exactly be out of character but miracle of miracles I resisted the temptation.

Don't be breaking out the congratulations just yet. There's bacon to be eaten here. I can flounce off later.

I watched him for a while but he just kinda sat there, hands on one of the stones, just... Touching it. Truth be told it was a bit weird.

Ok... There's only so long that I can watch some guy commune with a rock before even I start to get bored, so I got up to have a look-see. It was mind boggling to say the least. I mean... This WAS Temple Wood!!! It was in no way NEW, but it certainly wasn't old. It was different as well... The cists and cobble stones were missing, in this one at least, the smaller older circle just to the north already looked pretty much as it did in my time. I must remember to ask him about that later.

The Stones were still sharp and defined, hell I bet even the carvings... My thought tailed off.

The carvings!!! I tried to get my bearings... ok... There's that one... And that one... 1, 2, 3, 4, THERE!!! The spiral should be on that one!!

I'm certain THIS was the stone... But there was nothing... No spiral, no keyhole from which I had pulled the stone blade. Nothing. But that was weird. I mean, in my time, it was so weathered that it was literally almost faded to nothing. "I wonder..." Retracing my steps, I backed up a couple of stones, maybe the other one, the little concentric rings would still be there... It was! Is it weird that the first thought that occurred to me was that I had now seen this before any of the people in my own time? The surface of the stone was surprisingly smooth, and my fingers easily found the petroglyph... Tracing my fingers round its design...

"You want to be careful about what you touch in a place like this," a voice murmured behind me. I glanced back, a question forming in my mind. "It should be ok, I haven't completed the work yet but try not to make an offering, these things can be a little bit unpredictable."

"What do you mean? What IS this place? How did I even GET here??"

"Think Jen! You're thousands of years in the past. In a very real sense mankind has only JUST stopped being hunter-gatherers. How do you think we've travelled over such vast distances...? Crossed oceans...? Why do you think that there are cup and ring marked rocks to be found on every continent? Pyramids appear with monotonous regularity, remarkably similar in design, all over the world and yet it's put down to what your archaeologists call the concurrent evolution of ideas. There has to be contact Jen. CONTACT. Between people. Between cultures. The most infectious disease in the world is an idea. Spreading from person to person, culture to culture, from the past, into the future... And that, is what we do. What we did. We spread ideas. And we used these," he gestured at the stones, "to do it."

I gazed at him blankly. "Who exactly do you mean by WE??"

I swear he rolled his eyes so far back into his head he coulda probably have seen the last of the bacon burning over the fire. "Never mind that, I can see this is going to be more of a challenge than I thought, now, pay attention! I think it's safe to say that you understand that you can use the cups and ring marked stones to travel through time, yes?" I nodded silently, not trusting myself to speak. "You WERE paying attention, remarkable."

I could almost see his mind working. Judging me. Assessing exactly what and how much he could tell me. How much I would understand. Idly, he dragged his hand across the surface of the stone tracing circles. I saw it immediately in his change of posture when he'd decided to talk.

"Ok, how much do you know about physics? Anyone who has even a passing understanding should know that if you're travelling in time then you're also travelling in space, yes?" I nodded. "So, with a little bit of an adjustment, some tweaks, and a bucket full of imagination then it is possible to, instead of travelling from then to now, you can also travel from here..." He paused for dramatic emphasis... "To there. And with enough focus and understanding it is entirely possible to travel from here and now, to then and there, if you'll forgive the simplification."

"Are you trying to tell me that this is like a portal??Like a Stargate??"

A stargate?? Seriously?? I am on FIRE today!

"Do I look like I'm from the stars? No, it's just a relatively simple manipulation of the four-dimensional coordin..."

He tailed off...

Looking at me...

Judging me...

"Yes... Like a stargate."

I must have been standing there with my mouth hanging open because he sighed in what I thought was quite an exasperated way and returned to what he was doing. This was just way too much to take in. Bereft of any input or instructions from my frazzled brain, I did what I do best in such instances and walked off.

Chapter 5

By the time my mind caught up and had mentally remonstrated with my feet I was halfway across the field, heading for the cairns. There were a number of them dotted up and down the Glen, so much so that it is described as a linear cemetery.

Oh yeah... Check me with the knowledge.

It was really weird to see them complete and unopened. In my time they had been dug up, dismantled, rebuilt, and quarried. In fact, they were pretty much nothing more than mounds of stone. Landmarks in the landscape. Well, except the one at Dunchraigaig, that one always made me think of that chapter in Lord of the Rings where the Hobbits are lost on the Barrow Downs. That's pretty much EXACTLY how I imagine that looked. But these... They were still the silent mounds of stone that I knew, but it was kinda weird, even kinda creepy knowing that there was still someone, well, a body of sorts, in there. This travelling in time wasn't so bad. I could answer so many questions if only I could find someone to actually ask. I mean, it's not like he... Damn. Would you believe I didn't even know camper guy's name??

Aaaaaaanyway. The cairns. I could see them stretched out to my left, heading up the Glen past where Kilmartin would be in like a billion years' time, and down to my right... Down towards the Bullock Shed. Correction. Dow to where the Bullock Shed *would* be. That might be quite cool to see. The Ri Cruin cairn I mean, back in my time it had been pretty much destroyed. At some point in the past... Oh god, I mean the future... I mean...

Aaaaaaaaarrrrrgggghh!!!!! This is starting to bend my brain. Let's just agree to refer to everything in the never-ending present, yeah? At the very least it'll stop me having a grammar induced breakdown.

In my day, the ruins of the Ri Cruin cairn were hidden amongst the trees, destroyed by the early Victorians in their quest for riches. It'd be kinda nice to see it as it was, whole and unopened. I loved it more than the others 'cause it was the first place that 'adad had taken me on my first visit to the glen. It was also the first time I had managed to discover rock art. Now, when I say discover, I am very well aware that I didn't discover anything, but to my young mind I'd discovered them. That made them mine.

The trees were still there, and I could see what I'm assuming was the cairn peeking out from the clearing at the centre

Of course, I know they weren't the same trees. Jeez, give me some credit.

Oddly it was smaller than I'd expected. And it was open. How could it be open? We were thousands of years in the past. There was literally nobody here. How could it already have been desecrated? The panic which I had been successfully ignoring began nibbling at the edge of my mind again. I had thought that I was becoming numb to it, but all it took was a little thing like this to put me back on the edge all over again. I looked closer and it became more and more apparent that it hadn't been opened. In fact, it looked, to me, like it had never been finished. The cists were open and empty.

That's a stone sided box where they put the bodies, to you and me. A stone coffin if you will. I'm sure I've told you this before. C'mon people. Pay attention.

I looked down into the cist... Looking for the rock carved axe heads... Surely, they would be there... On the head stone... Nope. No sign. Not even an outline. How about that? I'm not sure I was even surprised anymore. Where there should have been a stone, covered with axe-heads, there was nothing. We were way past panic nibbling at the corners of my mind now. I could feel those spider legs crawling all over my skin, tippy toeing up my back.

Relax Jen. Breathe. This isn't going to solve anything. You are back in time. It's perfectly reasonable that some things will be different. Breath. Its fine. Slowly I felt it starting to recede. Not disappear you understand, but enough that I was no longer threatening to drown myself in useless panic. Colour me shocked but I didn't think running in circles sobbing was going to change my situation any time soon.

Did it ever? Ok. I am in control. I am calm. I am.

I guess it wasn't really THAT surprising. These cairns were supposed to have been in relatively constant use over a long period of time. Tens, possibly even hundreds of years. It was hard to imagine how, or by whom, they were used, when there was literally nobody about. No villages, no real signs of habitation at all. It was really weird looking at a landscape that was so familiar to me, but which had been stripped of almost everything that had made it so. No roads, no houses, and no villages. Weird. Just really, really weird.

What to do now? I still had time to play with and I was pretty sure I wasn't going to get any answers until he was finished with whatever it was, he was doing. Lacking a better idea, I just kept walking in the direction in which I was going, following what, in a couple of millennia, would become the old Poltalloch Road. Step by step it drew me down towards the coast, down to the old ferry.

Well, down to where it would be. Eventually.

******

It was always one of the more beautiful spots in the glen. When the tide was out it left a wide expanse of the mud flats stretching out across the bay with the narrow meandering channel of the river taking slow wide sweeps on its journey to the sea. There had been times in summers past when I'd walked from one shore to the other, the water being barely waist deep at low tide. I found a boulder and sat down, after a couple of minutes the sound of the waves had begun to work its magic, began to seep into my mind. It was such a soothing, almost hypnotic sound. Soon all thoughts of time travel were being washed away, to be replaced by a calm acceptance.

I was always more of a beach fan than a forest fan, the wind in the trees is all well and good but you just can't beat the whisper of waves on shingle.

You know that feeling you get when someone is staring at you? That kinda uncomfortable prickling feeling?? Yeah, that. I was having that in spades. I opened my eyes and there, about 20 meters from shore, was a boat. A small round boat. What did they call them?? Coracles??

Regardless. There was a boat, and in that boat, was a man. And he was staring. Right. At. Me. What in god's name was I supposed to do?? I did the only thing I could think of. I stood and waved hello. Shouting things like I meant him no harm.

Can you believe I actually said that? Me?? a 15-year-old girl telling this fully grown man that I meant him no harm?? Who did I think I was?? Queen Medb??

Whatever he made of my awkward attempts at friendship it was clear by his frantic backwards sculling that he didn't want to exchange phone numbers. I think, more to avoid causing him additional distress, I decided to head back.

The poor guy was currently spinning in circles... Don't laugh. You try rowing a round boat and see how well YOU get on...

Surely my host would have finished whatever it was he was doing and could answer some of my questions now. Which, I made a solemn promise to myself to at least try and ask in a calm, relaxed and coherent manner.

See? I was calm. Go me!!

The sun was low on the horizon by the time I made it back to the camp, and even from this distance I could hear the sound of stone on stone and as I pushed my way through the grass, I could see the source of the noise. He was on his knees, hunched over one of the stones... It sounded like someone striking a flint. That rhythmic sound of someone trying to coax sparks from stone. Tap... Tap... Tap... Sitting by the fire, I waited for him to finish. Eventually, with a roll of his shoulders he sat back and stared in silence.

There, faintly glowing in the twilight was a spiral. Well, not a spiral. Not really. More a nest of circles with a line scored through it... As I stared, the glow faded and finally died.

It actually looked like a mobile phone signal icon, but no way was I gonna tell HIM that.

"Who are you?" my voice seemed overly loud in the silence. He turned, and the look he gave me... Good lord, the look... It seemed to echo with a memory stretching back to the dawn of time. Strange eyes staring out from an even stranger face.

"I..." he sighed. "I am a relic. A traveller. I was the first and will most likely be the last. My name is Bran."

I couldn't stop staring at the spiral. This was the guy. I mean this was THE GUY who did the carvings!!! I can feel him staring at me, eyes boring into my face. Finally, I met his gaze, and the words came. "What's the connection? The spiral on the stone. My keyring. The tattoos. There MUST be a connection!"

He looked surprised, as if it wasn't the question he'd been expecting, but which had pleased him nonetheless. "The spiral??? In itself it doesn't actually mean anything, but the first of your kind who managed to use the portals had this as a tattoo. It naturally followed that those others who failed to duplicate his feat, believed that it was due to their own lack of a similar adornment rather than their own intellectual failings. As with all such things, belief has a habit of shaping reality and what started as an excuse became a reason and ultimately became accepted as fact. As a result, it's unlikely that any of your kind could successfully use the portals now without such a thing. It has in essence become a key and anyone who would use the portals needs to have the key. Most had it tattooed on their person since it's hard if not impossible to lose a tattoo. This however, he held up my keyring, "Is dangerous."

How does he keep getting a hold of that??

"This could enable ANYONE to travel in time. Anyone! You've no idea how much damage this could do. For safety's sake I'm going to need to keep it. Maybe even destroy it. It absolutely cannot be allowed to fall in the hands of those who would misuse it or by the goddess, someone like you who could end up hopelessly lost in time."

"But... But... If you destroy it, how will I get home?". He looked at me, "Jen, if you're going to be travelling through time then there is no avoiding the fact that you're going to need a key."

It took a moment for what he was implying to sink in. "You're talking about giving me a tattoo???? I laughed in disbelief. My mum might not have noticed I'd already been gone for nearly a day, but you can bet your last penny she would notice a tattoo. No way, no how. I shook my head "Sooooo not gonna happen. You shoulda seen mum's reaction when I shaved my head. If I went home with a tattoo, she would lose the plot completely!"

He shrugged. "It is of course entirely your choice, but it's the only way you are ever going to get home."

I sulked... Well, not really. I mean, I'd always thought about getting a tattoo but of something I'd chosen and in a place of my choosing, not some crappy spiral thing.

He was rummaging in his pack, "I'm sure I had the stuff in here somewhere... Ah yes, here it is." He pulled out something that resembled a long, pointy stick (!!!)

Now, when I said I'd thought about a tattoo before I meant I'd thought about the aesthetic of tattoos, not the actual physical process of having them done. For those of you not in the know THEY HURT. To a greater or lesser degree, depending on the person, but the common thread here is that THEY HURT.

After a couple of minutes rummaging, he also produced a small of pot of whatever it was he planned to use as ink. He looked at me, eyebrow raised. "It won't hurt, and it'll only take a minute. Trust me."

"Trust you? Are you kidding? First you tell me that you're not gonna send me home and now you tell me that you need to give me a tattoo. Oh, and in case you didn't notice that's a freaking stick!!! A stick for goodness sake and you think I'm gonna trust you? Did you bang your head? Why on earth should I trust you???

He just stared at me 'til I broke eye contact, "It's your choice Jen and you don't need to decide right now but understand this, you're not going home without one. Think about it. We can't do anything until tomorrow at the earliest. The portal needs to recharge…" He tossed me a blanket and motioned towards the fire. "Sleep whilst you can. Tomorrow is likely to be a long day."

Chapter 6

You will never really know how cold Scotland can get 'till you sleep outdoors with barely any shelter. Yes, I know I was thousands of years from home but guess what? It was still cold. And it was still wet.

Funny that.

And to top it all, it felt like I'd been sleeping on a thistle all night. My cheek felt like it had been stabbed or savaged by a cleg. Seriously it felt like the left-hand side of my face was about twice the size of the right. That's all I needed. I cast about, looking for something, anything, that would give me a good reflection, but there was nothing. I sighed in frustration. Don't get me wrong, I don't have what I'd consider to be a vain bone in my body, but at a time like this, the lack of a mirror was causing me something close to physical pain. Never mind, it's not like there were any people about to point out my sudden facial deformity. Bran was already up and about and breaking camp. Not that there was much to break, some blankets to stuff into his bag and kick dirt over the fire and we were good to go. He acknowledged my presence with a nod and a smile as I followed him out of the glade and headed out across the fields.

Hurrying to catch up, I asked, "Yesterday, when I was off wandering, I saw a man. Down by the shore? I didn't think there were going to be anyone else here."

He smiled, gesturing about himself, indicating the standing stones which littered the meadow. "Who do think built all this? They don't come up here very often and they give me the privacy I want. In return I try not to interfere in their daily doings. They are the Epwose. The people of the horse. They have been here for time out of mind. I think they might even have been here the first time I visited and that was a LONG time ago. For some reason they believe that the horse is divine."

"Is it? The horse I mean."

"Of course not" he laughed but I'm not going to tell them that. It's not for me to judge or criticise someone else's beliefs."

Feeling the need to talk I pushed on. "You said last night that we'd have to wait until this morning because we'd have to wait for them to recharge... What did you mean by that??"

He stopped and stared at the sky as if considering his answer, "I guess there is nothing to lose by telling you that much, the simple answer is that every trip uses up the energy that has accumulated." I stared at him blankly "You're not going to make this easy for me, are you? He said with a laugh. "Ok, now listen, Everything that happens uses energy. Grass growing. Rain falling. Wind blowing. People... Blessed Bel, You would not believe how much energy a normal human generates and uses on a day-to-day basis. Every living thing accumulates and discharges energy. The excess energy gathers in certain places. All around you. The planet is in effect a single giant capacitor." He paused, "You do know what a capacitor is, yes?" I punched him on the arm. "Ok... So, on the one hand we have all this stored energy and on the other, the fact that traveling in time or space, or both, needs a lot of power. All these so-called monuments were originally built, or more often, modified, to take advantage of all this free energy. The longer or farther you travel the greater the expenditure of energy but since it is essentially an endless resource it doesn't take long to recharges, unless of course, something is done to disable the location or if someone is stupid enough to use them at proscribed times."

"Proscribed times?" I Interrupted him, he smiled, "You're just full of questions today!"

I laughed, "I'm just making up for yesterday, normally I'm a pretty inattentive student, but this had hooked me. I wanted to know more and said as much.

"Well, there are certain times, days of the year, Beltane, Samhain, you know... Equinoxes and solstices, that kinda thing, when the barriers between worlds are thinner, and to use the portals at such a time could invite a bridge to form between realities. Believe me, that is not something you want to mess with."

"You're actually serious, aren't you? Different realities??? What like parallel dimensions and stuff??"

"Goodness no I mean different realities. Like Fairies and Demons. Heaven and Hell may well exist out there somewhere, but I guarantee you that they are nothing like what you imagine them to be. Same as Fairies aren't all small and sweet and live on milk and honey."

We were straying into areas where my scepticism was starting to reassert itself.

Elves? Really?

Not wanting him to clam up, I tried to change the subject. "So how is it that you know Callie?"

"Callie?" He pursed his lips.

"You know, the woman who sent me back here"

"Oh... You mean The Cailleach?"

"The what now?" It was my turn to be confused.

"The Cailleach, it means The Hag. I know that sounds a bit harsh, but it was the name which was bestowed upon her as a child due to her appearance. Her people were a superstitious bunch and someone with white hair and white eyes was always going to be viewed with suspicion and such was the case with her. It didn't take long for her to be branded as a witch. A hag. Eventually over time, her activities ensured that she came to embody the name more than those who originally named her could possibly have anticipated."

I looked at him in askance, "Your people are cruel Jen, especially the children. You inflict names upon each other. Names intended to hurt or demean without any understanding of the power that names can have. Ofttimes, you grow to fit the name, occasionally, the name moulds the bearer to fit it. The Cailleach was such a one. In the beginning she hated it but as the years passed, she came to embody it more and more until one day she gave up her birth name and adopted the Cailleach or, as you call her, Callie (or any number of variations) as her true name. As I said, it sounds harsh, but you've met her. You know her. Can you honestly say that it doesn't suit her down to the ground? She is as twisted a soul as I have ever encountered in all my years on this Earth. She and her companion, have been trying to disrupt the flow of history for hundreds of years, but then for some reason, something changed, and she started travelling alone."

He paused and I took the opportunity to fill the silence with some noise of my own. "Wait, you mean there are two of them?? What happened to the other one?"

He shrugged. "I do not know what happened to cause such division between them, all I know is that there was a disagreement and it ended with the two of them going their separate ways. I tried to track them but eventually he disappeared into time and ceased in his efforts to disrupt the natural order. Would that the same could be said of the Cailleach."

We were, as it turned out, retracing my steps of the previous day, walking, step by step, southwards. Heading back to Achnabreac. As we approached the river, it dawned on me. "Can't we use one of the other collections of carvings?? There are loads of them scattered up and down the glen, wouldn't the ones right here" (I nodded towards where Dunchraigraig would be in my time.) Work just as well?

"We could, if you wanted to go forward maybe 50 years, or mibbee 150 years give or take a year or two, but the ones up yonder…"

Oh my god... He used the word yonder, this guy was my hero!

"The ones up yonder…" he paused, "How to explain," he muttered. "The smaller ones are like your regional airports whereas Achnabreac or even Cairnbaan are more akin to your Heathrow. More accurate and more destinations. Plus, as I said earlier, the longer the trip the more energy required, and the bigger carvings have access to a greater store of energy.

"But none of that matters if I don't have a key, does it?" I looked down and sighed. I knew what I was gonna have to do. I think there was a fair chance that mum could learn to live with a tattoo if it meant getting me back in one piece. "Ok..." I said, "Let's get it over with. Is there a specific place where the tattoo needs to be?" Please God let me be able to get it on my back or shoulder or somewhere easily hidden

He looked surprised "What? Oh, my apologies, I was thinking about something else, one of these days I'll lose my head if I'm not careful"

"The tattoo" I repeated, "is there a specific place where it needs to be?"

"The tattoo?? Oh, don't worry about it, I took care of that last night while you were sleeping, I told you it wouldn't hurt."

Suddenly the burning prickling feeling on my cheek took on a whole new significance "YOU DIDN'T!!!!"

"Of course I did, where else did you think I was going to put it? You were lying on your arms, and you were under your blanket; your cheek was available. And frankly it's a place of power and influence so it will serve you better there than if it had been somewhere else. It marks you as a member of a very exclusive group of people. A family if you will. A Druid.

You've heard of the Druids? White robes? Mistletoe? Golden Sickles.? Yeah. One of those.

My hands were at my face, touching, feeling. It was tender right enough, felt quite hot. "What does it look like? What have you done to me?? Is there a mirror anywhere is this god forsaken time??"

He gestured to the stream, "Go look."

I dropped to me knees and stared down into the swirling water but couldn't even see a hint of a reflection. "This is useless!!" I cried in frustration. Muttering under his breath he stalked over. He leaned out over the water, and I swear he just glared at it. As if by magic...

That's right. I said it. Magic.

...it became as smooth and as reflective as a pane of glass. "Well?? He growled, "I can't keep it like this forever." I looked down and there I was, a perfect reflection, those weird eyes of mine staring back at me, I swear in some lights they looked the same colour as my hair, My red hair. Red... That doesn't really do it justice. It was ginger. I looked like a Disney Princess (you know the one). Thank god it wasn't curly is all I could say.

Did I mention that I'd shaved the sides? Yeah?? No, I've no idea why I did it either.

Not that the lack of curls in any way detracted from the "slept in the open and been rained on" style which I was currently rocking. I looked like some really annoyed war goddess or maybe a ginger medusa and there, on my left cheek, as clear as day and as delicate as a spider's web, was a little spiral about two inches across. It was really quite beautiful.

"Are you quite finished?" he asked.

"What? Oh, yes. Thank you." A day of time travelling and all of a sudden, I'm shrugging off all sorts of miracles.

He relaxed and the river started running again, slopping up over than bank almost in embarrassment and, incidentally, soaking my shoes.

Laughing, I retreated from the swollen stream, "You totally did that on purpose!"

He smiled and shrugged his shoulders, "Shall we move on? Moving off again and curious as always I asked," How did you do that? With the stream I mean." He shrugged. "When you get to my age, you learn a thing or two." He started picking up the pace, "It's not far to go but I'm not as young as I used to be, and I'd really like to get there before nightfall. I'm not a fan of climbing hills in the dark any more than you are."

I looked at him out of the corner of my eye and in all honesty, I would judge him to be no older than what? 30? 35? Never one to hold back I asked, "How old are you? I mean to my eye you look mibbee mid-thirties, certainly no older than 40."

He laughed. Like, one of those genuine infectious laughs? "Would it shock you to know that, by your reckoning, I would be accounted as being well over 4000 years old?

I stopped. Speechless. So shocked that even my feet stopped moving. I tried to speak but seriously there was nothing there to come out. I stood there, quite literally with my mouth hanging open. "How is that even possible?" I finally managed. He was looking at me with what looked like pity,

There was something about this guy that made me feel like I'd just climbed down out of a tree and discovered that I could walk upright but given the day that I'd just had I'd say I was doing pretty well.

"Let's just say that it's a side effect of the whole travelling in time" There was obviously more that he wasn't telling me, but my mind was still trying to process the whole 4000-year-old thing so I let it slide.

Finally, we reached the summit. I don't remember it being this long a walk yesterday but in all honestly there was a fair chance I was in shock, at least partially. Thankfully, today I had the chance to properly appreciate the view.

It was a clear evening and the glen stretched out before us. The sun, low in the western sky had turned the sea to liquid silver... Sending argent fingers questing along the rivers, turning everything it touched to gold. If ever anywhere had a claim to be the Summerland's of myth, then it was right here. Right now. Its beauty quite stole my breath away.

I looked back at him, the look in his eyes was far far away seeing a differing time. A different place. He sighed. "It's not home. But it'll do."

I turned my back to the sun, taking in why we had come. It was magnificent, so much more so than in my time. A huge panel of naked rock stretching off to my left and right, the entire surface was covered in spirals and cups and rings. Sooo many rings... Singles, multiples, large ones, small ones. Channels bisecting, joining, connecting. The design, if there was a design, was so complex that it seemed to draw the eyes, capturing my gaze. It was magical, in the true meaning of the word. "Did you... Carve ALL of this??"

He smiled, "What, THIS?" gesturing expansively? "Of course not, at least, I didn't do ALL of it. Bits and pieces, here and there. It has grown over time, new destinations get added, older ones become unusable though that's less of an issue here than it is with the Stones down yonder. Sometimes due to the number of incursions a particular time period becomes... Inaccessible." He shrugged. "It's a work in progress. Now, be still and let me look, it always takes me a wee while to get my bearings, It's been more than a few years since I used this one."

It was still kinda hurting my brain that I was standing here calmly talking about time travel with anyone, let alone some strange guy who claimed to be over 4000 years old.

Yes... He's strange. He is. Don't be fooled by his suave exterior and superior cooking skills. He's strange. You're forgetting what he did to that stream!

"Ok, I think we're almost good to go." He looked at me, his amber eyes seeming to catch fire in the gloaming light. You understand that I can't send you home? Well, I could, but there are things that you need to do first. I can only promise you that you will eventually return home."

My voice nearly broke as I cried out, "How can you promise that?? I'm only 15! I have no idea what I'm doing or where you're gonna send me! How can you possibly promise that I'll ever see home again?? How??"

"Genevieve, I wouldn't make this promise if I wasn't sure. When you were asleep last night, I had a look into the possible futures, and I can say with absolute certainty that you will eventually return home. But first, you need to make sure that you have a home to return to and I know, deep inside, that THAT is going to depend on you. You need to trust me, Genevieve. Time must flow, unabated, unaltered and the future must happen as it has always happened. Like it or not Jen you are a part of that future and even though you now exist outside of time, if you ever hope to return home, then you need to help me. We need to ensure that there is a home that you recognise, waiting for you to return TO. Do you understand??"

I nodded, mutely.

Of course I didn't understand, are you kidding?

"Now if you'll stand here. Right there. And watch what it is that I'm doing. Not just with your eyes but with your mind, your soul. Can you feel it??" The funny thing was, I COULD feel it... As he touched a cup here, dragged his finger round a ring there, I COULD actually feel it. Singing deep inside me, it was as though he were tuning the world's biggest xylophone. He was making music and I felt that if I could just see how to strike the right notes then I would understand what it was that he was doing and more importantly, how it was he was doing it.

His eyes locked with mine... Hand, hovering over a triple spiral, "Are you ready?" I nodded, tears threatening to spill from my eyes. He gently touched the centre of the spiral, and I felt my cheek burning...

My eyes flew open... I struggled, tried to move, anything to get his attention. I shouted... "What do you mean I exist OUTSIDE OF TIME!!???" He winked at me and everything just... Dropped.

Chapter 7

God my head hurt. Anyone who tells you that they would love to travel in time, see history, get answers, has obviously never been stuck in the past, with a headache and no pain killers. It's not the most pleasant of ways to spend your time. That said, I didn't feel sick this time which was a massive improvement on last time.

Time of course was pretty much front and centre in my mind right now with the biggest question being WHEN. When exactly had Bran sent me. It was dawn. Again.

Maybe it was just me, but it seemed like I had seen more sunrises than sunsets these last couple of days.

And you all thought NORMAL jetlag was bad?

Whether by accident or design, Bran had dropped me into a land, locked in shadow. Small constellations of light lay scattered up and down the valley floor like a reflection of the night sky and, judging by the fact that some were moving, there were people. Quite substantial numbers of people. I tried to recall anything that I'd read about this area in the museum or in my books but there really wasn't much information available for the period of time between the Neolithic and when the Romans started happy slashing their way across the country, and even then, it's not like they really wrote anything about Scotland that wasn't tainted with hints of sucking up.

What? C'mon, you know what I mean. The authors of anything written by the Romans, in Scotland, were obviously attempts at currying favour with a commander, a senator, an emperor. I mean, do you really think that the Caledonian General actually said:

"To robbery, slaughter, and plunder, they give the lying name of empire; they make a wasteland and call it peace!"

This was a man who probably shopped at Sheepskins 'R' Us and most likely carried a sword to the dinner table. Oratory probably wasn't in his skill set.

Aaaaanyway. Enough of my whingeing about the lack of books about Dark Ages Scotland, sorry, I should say Early Historic, my teacher would go mental if she heard me calling it the dark ages. She has a thing about it. Viking horns as well but we don't talk about that.

Seriously. Just don't.

By the looks of it some of those moving lights were heading in my direction so I stepped off the circles and into the shadows. I didn't have long to wait. The torches which they were carrying cast looong shadows in front of them, announcing their approach more effectively than any trumpet ever could. Moments later, as the sun crested the horizon, a party of men stepped into the light. They were smaller than I expected. I know it's an odd thing to say but people from the past gain stature in your imagination, until eventually they acquire the reputation of giants. People like Julius Caesar, Boudicca, Fergus Mor (It was even in his name!!) loom large, casting their outsized metaphorical shadows down through the ages. But these... You're lucky if any of them were my height and at 5'4 I'm not exactly tall. Feeling a little more sure of myself I stepped out into the light. The man in front looked me in the face, eyes widening and quickly touched his hand to his forehead then to his chest and bowed.

Bowed!!! I kid you not. A full-grown man bowing to me. ME!!!! That sorta thing could go to a girl's head if she weren't careful

He straightened up, "Failteachadh Sagart!"

That's "Welcome Priestess" for those of us who are linguistically challenged. Thankfully my inner google translate seemed to be working just fine.

He fixed me with a look that bespoke anything BUT respect, "It is long since we had someone arrive via the pathways. It is a strange day that I would give credence to anything that the Hag has said and yet a message came from her that a visitor had arrived here last night and would be in need of a guide. We have been directed to escort you to the citadel. You would give great honour to my house if you'd join us for breakfast. There is milk and cheese and bread, fresh from the oven this morning. Conall can go to the hives and fetch honey. It is not much, but the Draoidh are worthy of respect. You are welcome here." And with that he turned and started back down the hill.

I swear all I've done for the last two days is walk up and down this blasted hill. Up... And down. Up... And down. It was never ending. On the bright side my glutes were gonna look fabulous by the time I got home.

Circles and Stones

At the bottom of the hill, in the lee of a large boulder, they had tethered their horses. They swung up with practiced ease and waited patiently whilst I hopped round in circles trying to get my leg up and over the saddle horn. I should mention that whilst I HAD ridden before, what I was currently trying to mount most definitely wasn't a horse. At least, not in my estimation. It was closer to being a pony and if you looked at it head on it had the cross section of a barrel. (I learnt later his name was Curach) Finally seated, though not exactly comfortable, we set out. As I've mentioned, I'd ridden before, but it had been a couple of years and I could tell immediately that my thighs were gonna hate me tomorrow.

"How far do we need to go?" I ventured, He reigned in and waited for me to catch up before answering.

"My farm is at the bottom of the hill and along the river to the north, You can see it from here, the smoke rising from the fire pit, we can break our fast there before continuing on down the river to the hall of Ceann-Feadhna."

Still none the wiser as to where we were going, I asked "The Ceann-Feadhna?" he gestured and there in the distance, rising out of the mist like a whale breaching for air, was Dunadd. It all clicked together. We were going to the Hall of the Ceann-Feadhna. The Hall of the King.

******

As we rode, the sun climbed higher into the morning sky and I was becoming acutely aware that I had, to all intents and purposes, been wearing the same clothes for a couple of days now.

Or mibbee even hundreds of years. Same pants. Since the bronze age. How's that for a thought to put you off your cornflakes hmm?

I nudged Curach into a trot, something which I'm sure he hadn't done in, like, forever, and mindful not to kill my mount on our first day together I pulled up beside the leader. "Do you have anything I could change into to? Like clothes? I've been wearing this, I plucked at my jacket for emphasis, for days." He looked me up and down and grunted. I took this for an affirmation and smiled. "Thank you" This seemed to confuse him more than anything I had said, or done, thus far. Seizing the initiative with both hands I asked, "What is your name?" He looked distinctly uncomfortable…

Way to go Jen. Making guys uncomfortable aaaaall through time.

…"You want to know my name?" He sounded incredulous, as if no one had ever asked him this before,

"Well, how else am I going address you? People generally don't appreciate being called Hey You!!"

His face became sullen, and he dropped his eyes, "We are not required to like it, we are required to serve, to provide for your needs and to speed the Draoidh on their way.

"Well," said I. "I would like to know your name."

Turns out his name was Aed, and his wife and her family had farmed the land here abouts as bondsmen for 3 generations. It wasn't something that I'd ever really considered before, I mean I knew that Dunadd had been occupied as far back at the iron age, but it never really occurred to me about the lands round about. Kinda stupid really 'cause these hillforts or whatever they were called couldn't have existed without the infrastructure in place to support them. Food, drink, blacksmiths and what not. It's a whole society with Dunadd sitting at the centre like a spider in a web.

As so often happened with these things, those who lived and farmed the land in the surrounding area relied on the local aristocracy for protection and in return they provided sup and tuck for those at the top of the social pyramid. The farm itself was centred on a roundhouse...

An honest to goodness real live roundhouse!!

...Fields radiating out like spokes from a wheel, it wasn't so different to home if you chose to ignore the smell of peat burning or the circular nature of the surrounding landscape. There was even a scarecrow in the field we were passing, though, given the large crow currently sitting on (what I can only assume was) the head, its effectiveness was in doubt. I waved at it, more in the hope of scaring it off than anything else and it spread its wings and took to the skies. I watched as it flew, so much freedom exhibited in that one action. Down it glided, circling the approaching roundhouse once, twice, before settling on the peaked roof. I let my gaze lower, taking in the house and the courtyard and as we got closer it became apparent that all was not well and good. There were people. Lots of people. standing out front of the house. I could see Aed and the others straightening in their saddles, squaring their shoulders, sword belts being shifted round.

This was not good. This was not good at all. Aed glanced back, motioning to his men, who formed up on either side of me.

We entered the gate at a trot and pulled up sharply. There were raised voices coming from inside, suddenly Aed and his men were facing off against an equal number of others but who were much heavier armed. Things were absolutely about to go sideways when a voice cut through the tension and sent shivers down my spine.

"By the Goddess, I can't leave you alone for 5 minutes without some sort of fight threatening to break out" I turned, and there, sitting astride a white horse, was Callie.

******

I stared. Her hair was pure white and there was something odd about her eyes....

And the white robe was a definite look!

...but the face. I would never forget that face. A face which at this moment in time was staring at me with open curiosity. She turned to Aed, Your message took us quite by surprise, we were not expecting visitors of such an exalted nature or for them to arrive in such a manner. Especially one dressed in such strange attire. I think it would be better for all concerned if she were to come with me"

Nuh uh. Not. Gonna. Happen.

Aed had dismounted and had approached Callie, taking the bridle of her horse in his hand. "You are mistaken your holiness, I sent no such msg. Indeed, it is only due to YOUR message that I took my men up to the Wytches Stones this morning where we had been informed that our guest awaited.

I started backing up, the thought of going anywhere with this woman didn't fill me with the warm fuzzies but it didn't look like I had much of a choice. And what options I did have were narrowing very quickly. Unless something happened. And quick. Callie's suggestions would very quickly become orders and she most definitely had the men to enforce them. I could feel the panic rising in my chest. I cast my eyes about, searching for an escape. Aed, noticing my reaction, smoothly interjected "Perhaps the king, not wanting to trouble your holiness sent a message to me and simply forgot to tell you. I'm sure your holiness wouldn't want to countermand the kings wishes given that we were the ones tasked by the king with our guest's safety"

Her eyes flashed. "Are you trying to say that she wouldn't be safe with me?"

This was starting to get out of control, I'd seen first-hand how Callie could go from normal to scary beyond all belief in the blink of an eye. My presence here was going to get people hurt, possibly killed, I needed to get control of the situation and fast. I pushed down my fear and put myself between the two of them, "For the love of God Callie, would you just STOP??

She rounded on me, eyes blazing…

Oops.

…What did you call me?? She pulled a glittering knife from her waist and advanced on me. Aed pulled his sword and moved in front of me. "NO-ONE may address me as such!!" she shrieked, turning to her men she pointed at me with her knife. "Take her" This was getting ugly really quickly, I was trying to reason, trying to calm the situation but there was obviously something between these two and this was just the excuse they had been looking for to get into it. For the first time since I'd been dumped back in time, I felt completely overwhelmed which probably accounts for what happened next. I stood up in the stirrups and screamed…

The silence that followed was deafening and in that sudden silence, the crow had taken flight, and gliding down on stygian wings it settled itself on my shoulder.

If you thought it was quiet before, you should hear it now.

The silence was broken by the sounds of swords clattering to the ground, I opened my eyes and all around me grown men were dropping to their knees, hands covering their faces. The only other person in the yard still on their feet was Callie. Eyes wide, pale as sheet but still standing still proud, still defiant. I could see I'd made an enemy here today, She rode over, threading her way between the kneeling soldiers until she was level with me, leaning close she murmured, "You will address me as Your Holiness, Say it with me... Your Holiness... Say it!"

I could feel a prickling and looked down to see that she had a crystal knife pressed to my stomach. I swallowed, my mouth suddenly dry, "Your holiness" I whispered.

She smiled, the expression never quite reaching her eyes. "Try not to forget it."

She turned her horse, kicking her men to their feet as she passed. Berating them for their faint heartedness. "We will expect you at the citadel by the mid-day meal. Do not be late." She gave me one last look as she rode through the gate and was gone.

The crow nibbled my hair, bumped me with its head and took to the air. Aed was staring at me with something akin to awe on his face... When he noticed me staring, he shut his mouth and lowered his eyes, but when he lifted his head, he was smiling.

I'd made one enemy and one friend so far this morning. That wasn't bad going. Even for me.

Everyone was on their feet now and an awed babble filled the silence, Aed walked over and took hold of the bridle of my noble steed allowing me to gracefully slide out the saddle.

Ok... Now, when I say slide, fall is probably closer to the truth. Whatever it was, the word graceful doesn't even come close to describing it. Thank god Callie wasn't here or any shock and awe I'd just impressed upon her and her men would have evaporated like dew in the midday sun.

"My thanks learn-ed one." He said with genuine warmth for the first time this morning. "Your intervention was timely to say the least. We can generally look after our own, but we are not so well equipped that we could long withstand an assault by the hag's men." A woman came out of the house, a plaid over her shoulder.

They DID wear tartan!!!

Aed pulled her close, "Thank the gods you are unharmed. If it hadn't been for..." He paused and looked at me. Taking a deep breath, he asked, "Learn-ed one, might I know by what name you are called?" His wife gasped.

I looked around. This was obviously not something which was casually asked, I put my hand on his shoulder and looked him in the face. "Genevieve. My name is Genevieve."

He looked puzzled, his brow furrowed in thought, "Gwenhwyfief? Did I get that right?"

I laughed. "Close enough, now, about that breakfast which you promised me." His wife laughed. "For the saviour of the day I would produce a feast worthy of your deeds, but thanks to the tributes we must pay all I can offer you is bread and honey. Rest assured though, all that we have is yours to share. Come, your presence is a blessing on my house and will be a tale to tell the children. Bards will immortalise your deeds this day, Come." She took me by the arm, and I let myself be pulled into the roundhouse.

Aed and his wife...

I found out later that her name was Caoilin

...were as good as their word, I was allowed to wash and get changed, thankfully Caoilin and I were of a size, she was a bit shorter, but still, I was spared the indignity of looking like I was playing dress up in my mums clothes. My one concession was that I kept my boots. No way was I walking about in what passed for shoes in this era. The icing on the cake was the cloak she presented to me as we were leaving. A beautiful, finely woven woollen cloak. Something to keep you dry and to keep you warm at night she announced, and something to make you look like the Priestess that you are she whispered as she hugged me.

After much discussion it was decided that it would be better to arrive at court, just myself and Aed, a show of force probably not the best idea when dealing with the local muscle.

Aed hugged his wife as we left and if he held her longer and hugged her tighter than usual then no one was gonna question that. We were leaving home and hearth and heading into goodness knows what. If Callie had the King's ear, and I was assured that she did, then the goddess alone knew what kind of things she would be saying.

The goddess alone knew? Where did THAT come from? I think the time and the people were starting to rub off on me.

Circles and Stones

As the crow flies, It wasn't exactly far from Aeds farm to Dunadd, I'd even walked it occasionally in my own time, but the land was subtly changed. It's remarkable just how much you take the mundane things for granted. Phone signals. Cutlery. Drainage ditches. You forget just how much the fields of my time have been drained, how much irrigation has changed the landscape. I mean the Glen was a muddy place in the future but that was nothing compared to what the Moine Mhor was like here and now. I mean, I can literally see Dunadd. I can see the ramparts. Hell, I can even see people moving about but the route we were having to take to avoid the peat bogs meant that it was gonna take another couple of hours before we'd arrive. No way anyone was taking this place by surprise.

It was kinda odd, I was seeing what archaeologists and historians would give their eye teeth to see... The walls, the layout, the people. If it weren't so utterly mundane, I'd be excited.

Who was I trying to kid? I was totally excited.

"So, what's the deal with Callie?" I asked. Aed shifted in his saddle. "The Priestess? It would have been... On or about the shortest day of the year, when the fires burn all day. We'd had a local priest for a while, Old Cormac, but he died not long after she arrived. It wasn't suspicious," he assured me. "but he already had 53 winters behind him, and everyone knew his time was close. It didn't take long for her to get herself installed as the local priestess and even less time as the Chiefs counsellor. "Our society operates on a knife edge. It is a fragile balance that works only so long as both sides continued to follow tradition. At the moment the general feeling amongst the people is quiet anger. Something needs to change, or it will end in bloodshed, but at the moment there is no leader, no spark to set the fire. No-one will lift a hand against the priesthood and that's IF it is the Priestess who is responsible for the current troubles."

I looked crabwise at him, "I think it's pretty much a forgone conclusion that Callie is responsible for whatever is ailing the people of the glen." She is NOT a nice person."

Aed snorted, "I take it you have knowledge of her from elsewhere?"

"You could say that," I replied. "I thought she was my friend, but something happened and..." I lapsed into silence. I looked him in the face, "Let's just say that it's her fault that I'm here."

He frowned. Things are happening here that I do not understand. The attitudes of the people and the intrigue at Dunadd is just normal politics but you... And her... And that Bird? These things concern me. And there is that matter of the messenger. The priestess did not send the message, of that, I am sure. She is many things but a liar without cause is not one of them. I certainly didn't send a message to her, so the question remains, from where did the message come from? Who knew you were coming here?"

I shrugged. Only one other knew that I was here, and he was thousands of years away. At least, I think he was.

We rode on in silence and I took the opportunity to enjoy my surroundings, it's not often a gal gets to see the Iron age in action. Not that there was a lot of action. Actually, the closer and closer we got to Dunadd it'd be more accurate to say there was a lack of anything resembling action. Empty farms. Untended fields. Burnt out roundhouses. It was not a happy sight and dark thoughts began to fill my mind. Aed was right. Something was wrong here. Something was very very wrong.

Circles and Stones

Dunadd towered over us, casting a loooong shadow in the morning sun. We were approaching from the back and would circle round the base until we came across the path that led upwards. The whole time we were circling the base put us in weapons range and in danger of being used as target practice by any slingers currently occupying the walls. They knew we were here as we hadn't exactly hidden our approach and my cloak, blazing in the morning sun announced pretty definitively the type of person who was currently on the way to visit. Fingers crossed the traditions held true and that it was bad luck to kill a member of the priesthood.

I heard a harsh cry from above and looked up just in time to see a stone leave the sling of one of those on the wall. I followed its path and witnessed it miss, JUST, a bird circling in the thermals above the hill. I wondered... Could it possibly be?? I held out and arm, put the fingers of my other hand in my mouth and blew... The whistle cut through the air like a bronze knife through butter and the bird folded its wings to its body and dropped like a stone. A couple of yards above my head it spread its wings, arrested its descent, and settled, dramatically, on my wrist. This was a bird whose sense of the dramatic matched my own and together, under Aeds astonished gaze we ascended the path to the gate.

The guards at the gatehouse moved to stop us but took one look at the crow on my arm and dropped their eyes, in one case going so far as to drop his weapon and fall to his knees.

It has to be said, this could prove to be more useful than I initially thought.

Aed urged his horse forward, calling out "Make way... Make way for the High Priestess Gwenhwyfief!!!"

I swear I almost fell off Curach. High Priestess??? What was he doing??? Falling in with his plan the crow seized the opportunity to spread its wings and issue a call which rang out across the glen. Again and again, it cried out until the hilltop echoed with the harsh call of the crow.

Silence.

I could feel every eye upon me. Every breath baited. I sat there. Still. Focused. Unmoving. Face hidden in the depths of the hood. The Crow, perched on my shoulder now, was a patch of midnight on the white of my robe. A voice rang out from above. "You do us honour with your presence High Priestess" The Chief gazed down from his citadel and there standing behind his left shoulder, eyes burning with barely suppressed rage, was Callie.

She stepped forward and gazed down at us with imperial disdain, "It is rare indeed that we get such esteemed visitors, please, take your ease and we shall join you shortly"

I climbed down from Curach and hitched him to a post...

Rather more gracefully than I'd mounted him I might add.

...Becoming aware of the silence, I glanced at Aed, whispering, "What are they all staring at??" He looked at me as if I were crazy, "The Bird... You still have the bird on your shoulder!!"

"But it's just a bird!!! Hardly something that would frighten grown men into silence! He looked at me as one would a child. Birds, and those birds in particular are considered to be messengers of the gods or, on some rare occasions, to be the gods themselves. It is not unheard of for them to take another form. A dog or a bird or even a fish, to influence events in this world.

"What on earth was he chucking stones at it for then?" I indicated the guard on the wall who was now on his knees, his face pressed to the ground.

"I know not but I'll wager now he wishes that he hadn't." He said with wry smile.

I laughed and turned to the bird and spoke directly to it... May as well make a production of it... "You can go now, but I may have need of you later" It tilted its head to the side, as if it understood what I'd said and with a mighty thrust of its wings it was airborne. It circled my head a couple of times and, its wings beating the air, flew off towards the north.

Aed smiled and shook his head. "What," I asked, innocence oozing from every pore, "is it that everyone finds so frightening about birds??"

"People round here are farmers and fishermen and as a general rule are superstitious. They see something unusual, something unexplainable and before you know it there are stories and tales about it being told from one end of the glen to the other." He suddenly grinned, "It is not impossible that, after your performance here today, you could become a legend in your own lifetime" Turning serious again he continued. "In this instance that might not be the worst thing that could happen, indeed it may well be the only thing that will keep you safe from the wrath of the witch."

I thought I could see his point. That being said, from what I knew of Callie she was as likely to lash out as she was to be calm and reasonable. It remained to be seen whether the Callie of this time period was as restrained as the Callie of the future. It was a fine line to tread. I stood and waited whilst Aed secured his horse and we started to climb the long steps to the citadel. The hill itself was almost triangular in plan, with a broad courtyard to the southeast and summits to the north and west, upon which stood the citadel. We entered through a gate in the southeast corner, through a broad well provisioned wall. Following the path up past other structures which could have been stables or guard houses or even storerooms we finally entered, through another defensive wall until we stood looking up at the Hall of the King. This was a stronghold to be reckoned with and could, if held by a determined force, be held for weeks or, if there was a well (which I later learned there was) indefinitely.

The view from the top was as impressive as I remembered it. Over the Moine Mhor and down to the bay and further out, to the islands and beyond to where I knew Ireland to be. My eyes automatically looking for the landmarks which were so familiar to me, forgetting for a moment that it would be another couple of thousand years before the canal would be built. I could see boats pulled up on the sand and hear the suggestion of gulls on the wind. It was breath-taking. The sound of a gate opening dragged my eyes from the view and back to where it should be. Exiting the gate to the hall was Callie, upon seeing us she strode over, walking right past Aed she stopped before me. For some reason I seemed to remember her being taller but here we were, looking at each other eye to eye, almost as if we were equals.

"It's a fine view, don't you think?"

I remained silent, you never learned anything from not listening and if you listen long enough and hard enough then people will often say more than they realise.

"But I don't think you have travelled over such distances just for the view. I trust the weather was agreeable on your journey?" I looked at her in confusion, then it dawned on me. She had absolutely no idea where I had come from and more to the point, she had absolutely no idea who I was. I could be anyone. I could literally be the High Priestess for all she knew.

Circles and Stones

For the first time in days, I smiled and if that smile was a little bit smug then I'm sure you'll forgive me. In front of me stood the woman who, in a couple of thousand years, I would consider a friend, the woman who would casually throw me back in time and here she stood. Uncertain. Confused. Was it possible that she was even a little bit afraid?

I composed myself. Drew myself up and settled my face into what can only be called resting bitch face.

Maybe that should be rechristened resting high priestess face

I tried to put as much disdain into my voice as possible, "I think Callie," her face darkened at the name, "that I have seen enough. Please take us to your master."

She flinched as if I had slapped her, I'm not gonna lie, it was glorious to see but I put a gag in it and followed her through the gates and into the hall.

Into darkness.

Chapter 8

I was effectively blind, all around me I could hear noises, dogs barking people talking, whispering, murmuring, I started, strangling off a gasp as I felt a hand on my shoulder, "Relax Gwen, it's just me" Aed whispered. "Keep moving."

"Oh my god. What is that smell?" I muttered to him.

"What smell?"

"You mean you can't smell it?" It was so bad I thought I was going to be sick. A torch flared at the other end of the hall, and I could see a man sitting on a high seat.

Aeds voice came out the darkness. "Whatever you do don't pay him homage... You are his equal in rank and his superior in everything else."

I glanced at him, but he showed absolutely no sign that he had said anything. Finally stopping before the dais, I gazed up at the man sitting on it. Waiting in silence for him to speak.

The silence stretched out... Seconds into minutes until he smiled, as though he had divined some great secret. "Well, Aed, have you finally come to bend the knee and resume your responsibilities?

Aed stirred beside me, "We have wildly different ideas on what those responsibilities are father, and until you accede to my request or stand down from your position then I am content to live as I am."

Wait... Father? This was his dad? Oh, this was wrong on sooo many levels. Family disputes were never good (and almost always messy). This was obviously a discussion that had been going on for quite some time, and which stood, as yet, unresolved. He grunted, and now that I'd had it waved in my face, I could totally see it. In fact, it was remarkable just how similar they were and how closely their interactions reflected my own with my dad. It was all I could do to conceal a smile. "Enough," the king made a chopping motion with his hand. "It is too long since we have talked, tell me, how fares the gentle Caoilin?

"She fares well father, indeed, the goddess has blessed her, and she is with child. The purpose of my visit is thus twofold. To inform you of this joyous news and to deliver unto your halls this most eminent of guests. It was indeed a happy coincidence that your counsellors' message reached me ere I had left the farm, or I would have forsaken the honour of escorting this esteemed guest into your presence.

I was staring at Aed as if he had suddenly grown another head. Seriously... I didn't think it was actually possible to mangle a sentence like that. I think my tongue would have tied itself in knots had I even attempted to speak in such a manner.

Aed bowed, "If you will excuse me father, I must return to my wife ere the sun sets." He turned to me and murmured. "You will come to no harm in these halls unless it is from her." He indicated Callie with his head, "My disagreement with him is of a personal nature but that is all it is, a disagreement. She on the other hand would do ill to any and all who dwell here should it but advance her plans. Whatever they may be. Fare thee well Gwen. Should you have need of me, send word and I shall come, as fast as I can, to wherever you may be." And with that, he turned and was gone.

The hall suddenly felt a little bit darker, a little bit more intimidating and I suddenly felt like exactly what I was. A 15-year-old girl. Lost in time, with few friends and no family.

The King had risen from his high seat and come down to me. It was only when he stepped off the last step that I realised I was taller than him. By quite a bit.

He gently took me by the arm and guided me to the board where there were seats and food. "Come. Sit and Rest. You must be tired from your journey. It is a rare day indeed that we have reason to celebrate the arrival of a one such as you. A priestess of the highest order. It was a sad day when we heard that the Romans had destroyed the druids and that they were no longer to be found in the land of men. Any who claimed such a distinction thereafter were deemed to be charlatans and were dealt with harshly. It is become obvious to me that I was misinformed." This he directed at Callie.

Oh? Was I detecting a bit of dissatisfaction in the performance of the priestess?

Sensing an opportunity to drive the wedge just a little bit deeper, I responded, "That's not strictly true and although it is a fact that our numbers are few. There are still those of us who travel the land. Teaching, listening, helping where we can. There are at least three of us at present, possibly more, who are engaged in such efforts.

Three is right, isn't it?? Me. Callie. And her BFF...?? Yeah. Three.

"I myself have but recently completed my training..."

Well, THAT was a lie. Kinda.

"...And as such this is the first time that I have left the refuge of the oak groves of home." Callie was looking at me with confusion written all over her face, well, c'mon, it's not like I could just say hi, I come from the future. Come to think of it, that was the big question, wasn't it? Just when about in time were we? Were we AD or were we BC? Iron Age or Bronze age? Not that such definitions would have any meaning to these people. I was wracking my brains trying to remember the history of this part of the country.

I took a wild stab in the dark... "I am glad to see that, unlike your neighbours on the mainland, you have been relatively untroubled by the accursed Romans.

The king brightened at this. "Indeed, they have, as yet, left us untroubled. We are few and can be of little concern to such a people. We keep ourselves to ourselves and..."

Bullseye! So... Romans in Scotland. First century? Second?

"...the people flourish. No more are we threatened by war in the south, no more are our children taken from their homes and forced to fight in the endless battles of those cursed sons of Mil." I started... He smiled at my reaction. "Are you familiar with our story then?" Mutely I shook my head. "Sit then" he motioned to a seat at the board. "We shall eat, and drink and I will tell you the tale. How it is that we, the most fortunate of people, came to this land, then mayhap you can tell me of your travels, it is long indeed since I have left this glen" Seeing no other option, I made myself comfortable for, what I was almost sure was gonna be an incredibly dull lecture, but it was not to be, the king, whatever else he may have been, was an incredibly gifted story teller. He had already called for food, so I sat back and focussed on his voice, it was rich and deep, and I found myself caught up in his words. Obviously glad of an audience, even one as grudging as I, the King began.

"The bards sing of an age when a great tyrant slaughtered the flower of our people. They tell of a prince from the north, him of the golden hair, who refused to pass under the yoke. To protect what remained of his family and his people he directed that a fourth part should flee, and he bade his sisters son, Mil, to take ship and to lead his people north, lead them to a land forever beyond the reach of the invaders. But Mil was sore of heart and said that it could not be. He would in no way forsake his Captain. "Wheresoever thou shalt lead, there too shall I go. Whensoever thou shalt fall, there too shall I, for without you, all hope is lost." Thus, it came to pass that Mil bestowed the task of leading the people upon his three sons. All was made ready and in three great ships they set sail and in that time beyond memory they came to Ierne and have contested the kingship ever since."

He paused as a servant, a woman, appeared with food and drink. He rose and served me bread and wine(?) If nothing else, he was a courteous old soul. I picked up my cup and drank. And promptly went into an extended fit of coughing. Cappuccino it was not. He smiled and waited 'til I had composed myself before continuing.

"Every year those sons of Mil came and took those men and boys who were able and did war upon each other on the plains of the south. Generations passed and the land, no longer tended, began to sicken. Crops lay rotting in the fields and a pestilence ravaged our people. Year after year, this endless cycle continued until there came a day when Loarn, the eldest of three brothers, lifted his voice and cried. 'Enough! No more will we fight. No more will we live just to die for those Sons of Mil.' and so they gathered their kin, and in the deepest night of winter they fled."

He paused to take a drink before continuing "They fled north. Past the seat of Kings, they fled. Past the Sidhe. Always following the coast. Always moving north. For twenty days and twenty nights they travelled through that war torn land until at last they stood upon those Giant's Step's and could flee no further. Then stepped forth Loarn, my grandsire's sire, and he did raise his voice to the heavens and called upon the goddess to show them the way forward. That night they beheld a wonder. The goddess drew forth her sword and laid it across the sky, its blade pointing north, but there was still no way forward. Again, Loarn cried out to the goddess and again that night her sword pointed north. Great was the consternation, for they were farmers and hunters and there were none amongst them who knew how to travel the waves. A third time Loarn cried out to the goddess, and she did take pity upon their plight and sent amongst them a teacher, his amber eyes bespeaking a lineage older by far than theirs and he did show them the ways of the sea. How to craft ships which could cut through the waves and how to harness the wind. Ships were built and sails were rigged and, on a night, filled with a thousand stars they set sail. They followed the goddess's sword north and where that fiery blade touched the horizon, there they found this fair land of mists and rivers."

He paused, his eyes fixed on mine "Three generations of peace and prosperity we have enjoyed since we came to this fertile shore and until this year our people have prospered and have become strong. But something... He trailed off. The king passed his hand over his face and sighed. The old guy could tell a story that's for sure. He sat and gave a shrug of his shoulders. "I apologise for the length of my tale but in my heart of hearts I have always been a storyteller, had the winds of fate blown from a different direction I would have followed that noble calling, but it was not to be."

"Enough." He passed his hand over his eyes as if in sudden weariness. "I ramble, please, tell me how it was that you came to be here and how, if at all, I may assist you?" So I spun him a tale of dire warnings and prophecy and how a great evil was abroad in the lands and how it was my duty, indeed the duty of all, to find and if possible, eliminate said evil.

I really need to stop reading teenage fantasy fiction.

"I require very little my lord unless it may be that you have some out of the way place where I can meditate and continue my studies whilst remaining accessible to any and all who would seek my advice or my help."

"An admirable sentiment to be sure" he boomed, hand striking the arm of his seat. This man was incredibly enthusiastic, and I could see exactly how easy it must have been for Callie to gain such standing and influence in such a short period of time.

"I shall send runners to every corner of the Glen and beyond. A place shall be found befitting a High Priestess, and if none can be found then a place shall be built!" He stood and strode from the hall, calling his men to him, issuing orders. Leaving me alone, and the hall, in silence.

From the darkness, a voice echoed out to assail me, "Now, I'm thinking that everything you have just said, is a lie. Even if you had been selected for training, you would only barely be an initiate let alone High Priestess. I myself have stood before the masters so I can assure you that I know what I am talking about." The voice seemed to be coming from all directions at once. Echoing around the dark chamber, defying any attempt at locating where she was. "So, if you're NOT of the druids then the question remains... Who. Exactly. Are you?"

"I am who I say I am. I am Gwenhwyfief and I have come to find you."

"You came to find me??" she laughed. How could you possibly even know who I am?"

I took the opportunity to score some of my own points "I know exactly who you are. I've been told all about you. You're The Cailleach. The Hag. I know where it is that you come from, and I know what it is your trying to do. I even know why it is that you're doing it. I know everything."

Which, in case you hadn't noticed was a big ol' lie. Talk about over playing my hand

"And I have been sent here to stop you"

"You were... Sent?" She was on the offensive again,

You know what a facepalm is? Yeah. One of those. Big one. Huge.

I could feel her moving in the shadows, moving towards me... Her voice was getting louder, closer, more filled with anger. "YOU. WERE. SENT? And who exactly sent you hmmm?? Who is it that thinks they have the right to interfere with anything that I am doing? Not the druids, that's for sure since their power has faded in the land. Many years have passed since there were any with the power to stop me. So, if you weren't sent by the Druids the questions remain. Where have you come from and who exactly sent you. Everything that I've done has been for a greater good. Everything!!" She was shouting now. "No-one. NO ONE will stop me from finishing what I came here to do. No one can stop me from finding what it is that I'm looking for. Especially not him."

She stopped suddenly, a look of realisation dawning in her eyes. "That's it, isn't it? You were sent by him, weren't you? He's always interfering. Always poking around, always poke poke poke. Never facing me. Never revealing himself. But I'd know his style anywhere. Well. It won't work. Not this time. Not again. I will not be denied!!!"

She'd completely lost it, I took a step back... I'd heard that tone in her voice before. Right before her future self lost the plot and tossed me back in time. What is it they say? Never poke a bear? Even if it's in a cage it has the ability to turn round a tear your arm off and yet here I was poking the bear for all I was worth. When would I learn? I was looking around for a way out, I could literally feel waves of anger coming from her when another voice, right behind me smashed my already precarious calm into, like, a million pieces.

"You really shouldn't antagonise her. It takes forever for her to calm down again." I turned and found myself staring into the all too familiar eyes of my grandfather. I don't know what was more distressing. Finding him here or the utter lack of recognition in those icy blue eyes.

Yes, yes, I know, I should have seen it coming, I'm sure ALL of you did, let's just say I wasn't exactly firing on all cylinders that day.

"'adad..." It was the only thing I could persuade my mouth to say... I threw my arms around him. I just couldn't help it, It was probably the one thing I coulda done took him completely by surprise.

He staggered backwards... Staring at me in confusion, "'adad??? I know of no 'adad" he rasped at me. It hurt to hear such antipathy in his voice, but I shook it off. He was alive. I mean, he was... Is... Kinda... His eyes still wary of me he walked over to Callie. "I don't know what you think you know but you have no idea who we are or what we can do."

It finally clicked. This wasn't my 'adad. This was the man he'd been before. This was granddad waaaay before he'd become 'adad. Way before he'd even met gran. He had absolutely no idea who I was. It was suddenly painfully clear. His relationship with Callie. The fact that he was here in the past. Callie's antipathy towards him in the future. This was who Bran had been talking about. The other half of the dynamic duo. Well, mibbee not quite dynamic. Devious?? Dangerous? Aaanyway, you get my drift.

They were circling me like a pair of sharks... You'd think I was some kind of threat... Never one to let it lie I opted to try and make things infinitely worse for myself. "So, YOU"RE the other one?? I never woulda thought to see someone of your stature reduced to a minion of the Cailleach."

"I am no one's minion!!" he roared, knocking a bench to the floor. Jeeze Louise... What was it about these two and losing their tempers? They were both in front of me now, in front of the throne, that meant the door was behind me. I took my chance (and a leaf out of their book) and faded into the shadows. Once I was sure I was out of sight I turned and ran.

Out the hall. Across the upper courtyard, and through a gate... Not heeding where I was going, just listening to the voice in my head that was telling me to get as far away from the temper twins as quickly as was possible.

When I finally stopped running, I found myself standing in the smaller of the two upper courtyards. It looked so different to how it would look in my time, but one thing hadn't changed. There in front of me was a small expanse of bare rock. And on that rock, were two carvings: a deep bowl about ten inches across and the same in depth and the carving of a boar. I ran my fingers over it…

Hey, you never know.

…but there was nothing. None of the music I felt when Bran had done the same. I sighed in exasperation. Bran. God, I hope he knew what he was doing because quite frankly I had no idea what was going on here or what it was he wanted or needed me to do. I turned to the sky and shouted.

Screamed is probably closer. I wasn't exactly feeling calm and collected at this point in time.

"A little bit of information would have been good before you sent me here!! "

I imagined I could almost hear laughing… I turned, hoping against hope that he would be there. That he would be there to just sort everything out and send me home. But he wasn't. The crow just sat there. Laughing at me.

I couldn't have told you how long I stood there. Staring out over the bogs, It must have been some time because the next thing I knew I could hear a voice shouting. Calling for someone. It took me a minute to realise that it was me that they were looking for. That it was my name…

Well… The name that I had assumed.

…which they were calling. This secret identity thing sure took some getting used to… I waited until I could hear footsteps behind me before turning to confront my addresser. He was a boy, well not quite a boy but not even close to being a man if I were any judge. I caught him staring and he hastily dropped his gaze, "I am to show you to your lodgings Holiness"

Holiness. I am NEVER getting used to that. I certainly didn't feel particularly holy right now.

I gestured for him to lead on, this kid looked barely older than 12, 13 at a push (turns out he was actually 14). I thought a bit of information gathering wouldn't go amiss. "Have you served here long?"

Really??? Jeez it was like a hop skip and a jump away from asking him if he came here often. Way to go Jen!! Sometimes I amaze even myself.

After I'd mentally removed my foot from my mouth I continued, "I was just wondering about the rift between your Lord and his son, and how such a state of affairs came to be?

"He looked about, "It's not really my place to say" he began…

I smiled at him. "Oh, come now, if you can't tell ME then who can you tell? I won't tell, I promise." I offered him my hand and after what seemed like way too long a wait, he took it and a bargain, and dare I say it, a friendship, was struck.

"It all really started when those two appeared. I was pretty sure he was referring to Callie and Co. Before that he was a just and able ruler but when they arrived, he offered them a place, as is required and they just never left. After old Cormac died, she was appointed as priestess and counsellor and his judgements became…" He paused, obviously struggling for words, "became… Unsound." The people began to grumble, crops were less than they should have been."

"But that is hardly the kings fault, is it? I said. "If the judgements are hers then surely the blame should lie with the priestess?"

His brow furrowed in thought before he continued, "The land is the King, and the King is the land. The priestess says that the goddess is displeased. In times gone by the simple solution would have been for the king to offer a sacrifice to the goddess to appease her wrath but now it is judged to be the people's fault. He demands more and we are forced to make up the shortfall from our own share. Tributes have always been the way, even before we fled the homeland, but they get higher every year. What was once a tenth part of everything is now half. People are leaving, those who object... Disappear. There are stories. Horrible stories. The prince tried to reason with his father but his was the lone voice. Drowned out by the bad counsel the king was receiving and now there are whispers of war, of invasion from our neighbours to the east." He looked about, as if scared he had said too much, as if the very walls had ears. With evident relief he led me from the fort proper and out into the lower ward where there were buildings, gesturing to the first one we came to and meeting my eyes for the first time he said, "We are here." I pushed the door open and stepped inside.

So, shoot me. I was excited. It was roundhouse for goodness sake. Yes, I know, I'd already been in Aeds but it's not like I had the chance to snoop around. C'mon, where are your manners?? This one was mine for the day, tell me you wouldn't be excited too?

There was a large circular room right at the centre of the room where a fire smouldered in the hearth, the smoke seeping up through the thatch. The rooms were separated from that central space by walls radiating out like the spokes of the wheel. In one of these rooms there was, for want of a better word, a cot. I turned, smiling all over my face, "This will be perfect, thank you." He looked quite startled. These people obviously didn't get thanked for their efforts very often (If at all!) I filed that little bit of information away for future reference. A little bit of gratitude in the right place at the right time, would quite probably go a looooong way. He left, glancing back once or twice as he went, confusion written all over his face. I sank down onto a bench beside the fire and let out an almighty sigh. It had been a very long day.

At some point I must have fallen asleep, mind and body fatigued from the stress of the day and lulled into a deep slumber by the soft cracking of the fire. My mind just seemed to drop, falling further and further down into that deep dreamless sleep.

Well, I say dreamless... I found myself aware and inside my mind. It's an odd sensation to be sure. Totally asleep and yet completely aware, I looked around the grey expanse that stretched into infinity, half perceived shadows moving in the corner of my eye. In front of me a shape began to grow, A lumpy unresolved object of almost sinister aspect. As it gathered more and more substance to itself, it began to resemble a fallen tree. Reassured, I started to really look about. It's not every day you get to explore your own mind, and when I turned back, calmly sitting on the tree as if it was the most normal thing in the world, was Bran.

"This isn't a dream, is it?" He smiled and motioned for me to pull up a branch. "Well, it is, and it isn't." Yup. Definitely Bran. He waited for me to get comfy before continuing, "Given the nature of time, I have a fair idea of what you would need to know and, more importantly, what it was you would be most likely to ask. This enabled me to create this simulacrum in your mind to answer all the questions which I considered most relevant to your situation. It was the work of mere minutes and was accomplished whilst I was rummaging about in your memories back when we first met..."

He looked like he was about to start getting all kinda quantum on me, so I interrupted him as soon as he paused to take a breath, "What did you mean when you said that I now exist outside of time?"

If ever a figment of my imagination could look uncomfortable then Bran was really nailing it. "It's a side effect of your travelling in time. The gods can't allow time to be disrupted. Things must happen in the order which has been determined. If you're going to travel in time, then you can't be a part of it. If you think about it, I'm sure you'll understand why. It is the only way to ensure that you can't disrupt the great tapestry. He paused before continuing, "Truth be told, I always thought of it more like a great river, but I was out voted. Basically, the moment that Callie threw you back in time, she removed both your ability to influence time and times' ability to affect you. Not something which she intended, I'm sure."

"But what does that mean??" I whined.

I did. I admit it, I whined. Even I can be a bit petulant when I want to be. It's not big and it's not pretty but it does sometimes get results.

The image sighed. "It means that you don't age. So long as you continue moving about in time you will remain exactly the same age as you were when you dropped yourself on my doorstep. Not only does it stop you meddling, but it means that when you do eventually find your way home, you're not suddenly 20 years older than when you left. I'm pretty sure even your dad would notice if you came home and were suddenly 35 years old and he's not exactly the most observant person in the world. Now is there anything else you absolutely need to know because dawn is not far off, and someone is about to knock on your door."

Circles and Stones

I awoke with a start... Someone was, in actual fact, knocking on the door.

Actually, they were knocking on the door frame. It's kinda hard to knock on a leather drape. I know. I've tried.

I stuck my head out from behind the "door" to discover that it was my erstwhile guide from the night before. "The king has news and requests your presence my Lady."

"Give me a moment," I went to pull my head inside when my stomach nudged me for attention. I stuck my head back out. "You wouldn't happen to have anything to eat now, would you?"

He grinned and from inside a sack he produced a loaf of hot bread, the smell instantly making my mouth water, and a block of cheese. "My mother said you'd probably be hungry and wish to break your fast, so I stopped by the kitchens and the storehouse on my way"

I snatched the food. "Your mother is a queen amongst women!! Give me a moment and I will be right with you."

I ducked back inside and tried to make myself presentable. The bread was barely recognisable to someone who was used to the stuff you buy in a supermarket, and it was... How shall we say... A little bit bland? The cheese, however. OMG. I needed to get my hands on more of this. My hair, as always, was doing its level best to look as if I'd stuck my finger in a socket and my face was smudged. Using the basin provided I dipped water from the barrel and washed, dressed, and threw my cloak over my shoulders and feeling a bit more human I stepped from the relative safety of my hut. He was still there. Waiting. He smiled as he saw me. I gestured grandly, "Lead on MacDuff!!" He took a step backwards mouth dropping open. Thinking I'd somehow offended, I rushed to reassure him. Forgive me, my friend, I meant nothing by it. Why don't you tell me your name? That way, we can start anew, and I won't keep making mistakes.

"I have no name holiness. I am the youngest of five, so even amongst my own, I am simply Balach...

That's "Boy" to you and me. This kid didn't even have a name!!

"Someday perhaps I may do something considered worthy enough to be granted a name, but until such time I shall remain, simply Balach.

I'm sorry ... what??? I was aghast. "Who decides if you have done something worthy of a name?? Everyone deserves a name! It's the only thing in life that truly belongs to you!!"

He shrugged his shoulders, "It is of no moment holiness"

I put my hand on his shoulder... "Is it within the power of a priestess to grant someone a name?"

"It is within the power of a priestess to do whatever she pleases my Lady"

Mind made up, I touched him on the shoulder, "For your aid in my time of need and for your honesty and friendship I grant you the name of MacDuff. From this day onwards you shall be known as Balach MacDuff."

You'd think I had just shot the poor kid, tears threatened in his eyes... "Look" I said, "I know it's not great deeds of swordsmanship and fighting in battles but sometimes it's the little things that count the most. Be nice to your neighbours. Help if someone needs help and give with no expectation of anything in return and people will remember your name for far longer than if all you've done is stick a sword into another person. Keep doing what you're doing, and you will earn that name, and my respect, a thousand times over."

He grabbed my hand and pressed it to his forehead… "I am your man Priestess!!! Call me and I will come." He turned quickly, tears on his face and without further comment led me to the great hall.

We paused at the great door, "How should I announce you?"

I made a decision and the moment I'd made it, it was as if something clicked in my mind, like a key turning in the lock and opening a door to a whole other life. "Announce me as The Lady Gwenhwyfief, High Priestess of Epona." I could hear the last echoes of his announcement being sucked into the silence as I stepped into the hall.

It was surprisingly bright, and I noticed the sunlight streaming in from windows, unshuttered, on either side of the throne. There was no-one there but for the King. I approached warily, not sure of the man I was about to encounter. From my encounter with him yesterday he had appeared to me, a man who was struggling with a job for which he was woefully unsuited and which, truth be told, he didn't really want. Such a situation will most always lead to mistakes, but he certainly hadn't appeared to be a monster. About halfway down the hall he rose from his high seat and came to meet me. "Come your holiness, walk with me. Off with you Balach, the lady is safe in my care. We exited the hall and headed down towards the lower courtyard to which I had fled yesterday afternoon.

Yes, I fled. I'm not too proud to admit it. You would have fled too if you'd been confronted by those two…

"What have you done to young Balach? He seems to have grown in stature overnight."

I glanced back and there he was trailing along not twenty paces behind us. "He showed me a great kindness and helped a stranger in need, so I bestowed upon him a name."

The king was startled. "A name???? Oh ho!! Names have power to those who know them" he paused, "and to those who know how to use them. Still... things may be looking up." The king turned and beckoned to him "Do you fully understand what this means? You are her man now. Where she goes. You go. Do you understand? With a name comes certain responsibilities, to your Lady and to yourself. Do not dishonour your name Balach, it is a stain that is hard, if not impossible, to leach out. Do yourself, and your patron proud or you will answer to me, and then you will answer to your ancestors." He turned back to me, "Your holiness, I have found you a refuge, it is farther north than I would have liked and is close by the wytches stones. It needs some work to make it habitable, but the walls are sound, and it is yours. I don't want to seem inhospitable, but you must leave and t'were best you leave soon before certain others take an interest in your whereabouts. I shall send message to those I can still command and shall let my son know where it is that you bide but you must leave, and you must leave NOW. Good luck my lady. Think not overly ill of me, I am in a bind of my own making, but your presence has given me something I have lacked for many seasons. Hope. You have given me hope. Balach, attend your lady."

Chapter 9

What the king had found was an old farmhouse. It sat not a million miles away from where my granddads cottage would be in the future, so the feeling of coming home was a pleasant surprise. The roof was gone and the land surrounding it was overgrown to the point of wilderness. It was small, but for the foreseeable future, it was home, or, at least it would be as soon as we'd cleared the brambles away from the doorway, at least, I think they were brambles, oh, and dug a toilet. Didn't think of that huh? Well, let's just say that at that moment in time my body was reminding me. Forcefully. That we had no WC.

As the days passed and turned into weeks it became apparent that like all 14-year-old boys, hygiene was not exactly high on the list of Balachs priorities. Something that changed the moment that his mother arrived.

It was always going to be a massive job getting this place liveable and after weeks of toil I looked at what we had accomplished and what lay before us with a growing sense of despair. Quite frankly if it hadn't been for the seemingly inexhaustible enthusiasm of Balach then I would have packed up and gone home. Metaphorically speaking of course. The hardest thing to get my head round was Balach. I mean, he was just a kid. He was even younger than me and even I was struggling with the whole living on my own thing. But here he was. Every day. Out there, digging, building, repairing. The fact that in the here and now, society considered him to be as much of a man as Aed, with all of the attendant expectations and responsibilities, really messed with my head. It took some time, but those weeks where we, with the aid of the locals (arranged by Balach I might add) re-thatched the roof and cleared the weeds from the land completely disabused me of the notion that he was anything but a very capable young man.

We were sitting round the fire in front of our tents, waiting for the mist to clear when the sound of a horse drifted out of the gloom. As it drew closer, we could hear the creak of a wagon's wheels, one of which obviously needed some oil...

Or whatever it was they used to lubricate a squeaky wheel back now.

A couple of minutes later, first a horse, then a wagon, then the driver resolved themselves out of the fog. Balach took one look at the driver and ran. I kid you not. He just got up and ran in the opposite direction. Awesome. Fingers crossed my visitor didn't have anything nefarious in mind. The figure approached me and when it was close enough to touch, the hood was pulled down to reveal a woman, a smile on her face. "That wouldn't have been my son who I just saw running down the field, would it?"

"Wait... You're Balachs mum?"

She looked confused, "Mum?"

Another adjustment I was being forced to make. Modern contractions just didn't work in the past.

"His mother." I corrected myself.

"I have the misfortune of bearing that burden." She said it with a smile and from the stories that Balach had told me I had no doubt that she meant it as a joke. She cast a critical eye 'round our, rather haphazard, campsite and shook her head, "I've taught him better that this."

I moved to help her down from her seat, but she waved me off with her hand. "That is not your place your Holiness." I stared at her, not quite understanding what it was that she meant. She jumped down and guided me to a seat. She looked at me. "I have heard tell of you from my son and from Caoilin, but I would fain hear from your own lips. Who are you and why are you here?" I looked at her, my confusion fading as quickly as it had appeared. Standing before me was a woman whose sole purpose here was to protect her family, or what was left of her family. "I ask you again Holiness, will your presence here bring harm..." Her gaze strayed in the direction in which Balach had so recently fled, "to the Glen..."

I stood and approached her. "It is not my intention to bring harm to anyone in this valley. Especially to any of those whom I consider friends." I took a chance, "or family." For that is what Balach was quickly becoming. In the last couple of weeks, he had taken the place of the brother I never knew I wanted. Every time I asked him to do something or help me with something he would reply with "I am your man Priestess," but the truth of the matter was, that with every day, he became more and more my friend, and I would protect that friendship and that young man with my last breath, and I said as much to his mother. The fierceness of the hug in which she caught me quite took my breath away.

I mean literally, I may have even made an involuntary squeak as all the air whooshed from my lungs.

We worked, we ate, we even laughed, and the days passed as days do until one morning, we emerged from the tents to find that it was done. There were no more walls to build. There was no more thatch to lay. I breathed a deep sigh and marvelled at what we had accomplished. I looked upon that which was to become my home.

And for a lot longer than even I had ever anticipated. Even in the dark days to come there were times when I found myself returning here, both physically and mentally. It was truly a place of peace.

The other part of the kings gift, in fact, the part which I have no doubt inspired him in the first place, was the cell. No, not like a prison cell... How to explain... It's basically a small circular building made of stone, every new layer of the walls ever so slightly overhangs the course below until they touch. It's called corbelling and produces a building that resembles a beehive. That's how they acquired their official name. Beehive Cells. Mainly 'cause they are shaped like beehives. Not the wee houses you see that people have at the bottom of their gardens. You know, like the kind you see in cartoons.

The king had obviously seen this little cell as the ideal place for me to become the glens own personal anchorite, or whatever this time periods equivalent was. Hermit? Somewhere and someone that the ordinary people could come and visit, chat, have their problems solved. Essentially, what he had done...

And quite deliberately I might add,

...was set me up in direct opposition to Callie. He had created an alternative power centre away from her, away from the citadel. Don't get me wrong it was a pretty astute piece of political thinking, and it changed my opinion of the King quite substantially. I grudgingly admitted to myself that maybe, he wasn't the buffoon everyone took him for, but I was just a wee bit concerned about how Callie was gonna to take it. I'm willing to make a pretty large wager that it was going to go down like a bag of sick.

Each morning and evening I spent an hour in the cell, in what Balach, and his mother came to call my quiet time. In reality I was sitting, or truth be told lying, eyes shut, learning from my erstwhile inner teacher.

There is possibly also, just the tiniest of chances that I MAY have spent at least some of the time sleeping. You would not believe how early these people got up. When they said they rose with the sun, they really meant it.

Anyway, back to the matter at hand. My inner Bran. He'd claimed that he'd only managed to give me a fairly limited list of answers to some fairly basic questions, but I had yet to find anything to which it couldn't provide an answer. My knowledge of the history of these islands and the history and use of the stones and circles expanded dramatically in those weeks and I grew more confident and assured in my assumed roll as Priestess. I quietly dropped the whole "High" part as it was only ever really intended to irritate Callie and it was an eminence I neither sought nor desired. This morning I was taking a break. I'd been listening for about an hour as Bran tried without success to explain a particularly difficult concept involving the nature of time but no matter how often he explained it I just couldn't grasp what he was trying to say. Eventually I opened my eyes in resignation and moved outside. There was a gentle breeze moving through the fields like a giant hand causing the crops to bend and sway, the sun was shining down and there were butterflies dancing in the air. It was a truly beautiful day. It dawned on me that I'd been here now for 6 weeks. People had a habit of dropping by, initially, I think, just out of curiosity...

Hello!!! Square House! Of course, they were nosey.

...but more and more they came seeking advice. Not that I was exactly qualified to give it but with the aid of Balachs mother everyone left in a better place than when they had arrived. My reputation continued to grow but in reality, it was Aoife who was doing all the heavy lifting.

That's Balachs mother by the way and no I wouldn't have known how to pronounce it either if I hadn't already heard it spoken out loud. Its Ee-fa. EE-FA. Got it? Good. Getting someone's name wrong is really bad form.

As a result of this I was speaking Gaelic every day and with nary a thought as to just how remarkable that was or any real understanding as to how it had come to pass. I'd even started thinking in the language and you have no idea how weird that is until you experience it. Mentally I made a note to ask inner Bran next time I saw him. I refused to believe that I was quite that gifted with languages. If, however my sudden proficiency was down to Bran then, given that it had first afflicted me in the future... Well, let's just say it would raise some interesting questions.

A shadow fell over me and I looked up to see Aoife standing there. "You," she started, "should be wearing a hat. You're not going to look terribly holy when your nose starts to peel."

I smiled sadly at her, "you sound like my mother."

She sat and put her arm round my shoulders. "She must be incredibly proud of the woman you have become"

I shrugged, "I've no idea, I think I've always been a bit of a disappointment. She and my dad generally don't have a lot of time for me, so I spend most of it entertaining myself," Books and history had saved me more often than I cared to admit, even to Aoife. I looked at her. "Making friends isn't something that has ever come easily to me, they were... Are... Few and far between. It wasn't exactly the greatest of lives but then my only real friend... Well... Let's just say that it's her fault that I'm here. Alone. Again."

I felt her arm tighten around my shoulder. "You're not alone Jen," I started at the sound of my actual name, "So long as I'm here, and Balach's here, you will never be alone. You will always have a place with us." At that point the waterworks really got going and I just couldn't stop. Until that moment, I'm not entirely sure I realised just how scared I was. Just how alone I'd felt. We'd been busy. My mind had been occupied with the cottage and everything that entailed. Even digging the ...uh... outhouse had been a pleasant distraction from my fears. Then the whole learning with Bran but here on this summer morning with nothing to do, it all came rushing back. I'd tried to hide it, but Aoife saw. Aoife had seen it all. The loneliness, the fears, and she had done the one thing she instinctively knew would help. She had quite simply extended her family to include me. She held me there until the tears stopped, wiped my face, and ordered me back to the house for a hat.

The hat thing aside I went to bed that night calmer than I'd felt in weeks and wonder of wonders I slept. There was no waking up in terror in the middle of the night and thank the goddess no nightmares. As a result, I awoke the following morning bright and early and without the ever-present headache which had plagued me since I arrived in this time period. I was even gracious when Aoife stuck her head into the room and told me to get up and dressed.

Suitably attired I helped myself to the pot of porridge that was hanging over the fire pit. I'd never really been a fan of porridge...

The food tasted different. Even familiar things like Porridge tasted different and, well, it still wasn't exactly my favourite thing.

...but when it was all there was to eat, well, you know, beggars can't be choosers. I was sitting at the table when she returned. "I think we're going to need to go to the market, I'd forgotten quite how much Balach eats. I swear he needs to start growing up or he is definitely going to start growing out." This last, she shouted in the direction of his bed and received a muttered response. She paused and I looked up to see her staring at me, "Do you fancy a wee trip to the market your Holiness? At the mention of the market, I'd perked up, there were things a girl needed and, well, If a girl couldn't get them then a girl was just gonna have to make them herself. The lack of soap was causing me something close to physical pain. Washing in cold water and scrubbing with sand was all well and good in a survival of the fittest situation but I wanted hot water. I wanted soap. Maybe even the odd scented candle.

Ok. So, the candle may have been pushing it a bit but thanks to my mother I had the basic knowledge of how to make soap. Oh... And dandelion tea. I might even thank her when I get home. IF I get home.

She was looking critically at me, "It'll do you the world of good to get out and about, beyond the limits of these walls. That, and it'd do no harm for the people here abouts to get used to the sight of your face."

Which was how I found myself riding, to the market, perched on the front of a wagon beside Aoife. And yes, it was raining. Raining in that very particular Scottish way. Not so much individual drops falling from the sky, more like the air itself was wet. Too thick and heavy to be fog. Not quite enough to be rain. Just the perfect amount to leave you soaked to the skin and with water dripping off the end of your nose.

"When I get a chill, I'm totally blaming you" I grumbled. She laughed. I kid you not, she laughed. She didn't tell me to stop moaning. She didn't ignore me. She laughed at me. I looked at this woman who had, inch by inch essentially adopted me. She'd had five children and had raised at least one of them on her own... "Can I ask you something?" Without waiting for an answer, I ploughed on "What happened to your husband?"

She laughed again, "Husband? Oh, we weren't married, we just kinda came together and stayed that way. Oengus never stopped long enough for us to make it official like. Always off on another adventure. Fighting in another battle. It's a wonder we had time to have children at all."

I thought she had stopped, but she continued. "It was eight, maybe nine years past, and our lord was in the middle of a disagreement with those men of the north and my Oengus was coming home from the Islands. The boats were overtaken by raiders. He did not survive. Balach had only 5 summers, and my other boys were not much older. His lordship was kind enough to employ me and give us shelter."

"And you've been alone ever since?"

Way to go Jen. That wasn't insensitive at all.

"Goddess no" She laughed. I had my boys with me whilst I grieved for my man as is proper and then I moved on, as he would have wished me to do. There have been others, but

119

none as I would invite to share my hearth. None but one." And with that she would say no more, instead turning my question back on myself. "How is it that you know the Hag? From what little I have heard, there is little love lost between you. And I don't just mean directed from her to you. She has always been of a malicious disposition but you... I see an anger in your eyes when you talk of her. It is not good to hate something or someone with such passion, it will always do you wrong. What I see is not the hatred born of impulse. It is a hatred born of experience. Of betrayal. You and she have a past that you aren't telling us. So, now that it is just the two of us and I have shared something of myself, tell me, how is it that you know the Hag?

Just how much should I tell her? I mean... Time travel... Bran... Magic?

C'mon, this was Aoife. If I couldn't trust her then I couldn't trust anyone.

I shrugged and looked away, at the fields rolling past, "She was my friend. She was my friend when I most needed one. When my grandfather died, she gave me a safe place to grieve. Gave me the chance and the time to adjust. She never asked me for anything, but she was there if I needed her, but then... I'm not sure what happened. Things changed. SHE changed. I can't pinpoint what it was that I'd done but just like that," I snapped my fingers, "She changed. We were going up to the circles... The stone carvings like the ones above Dunadd," I explained at her look.

She frowned "The wytches stones? They are ill omened places, haunted they say. People who have lingered there over-long have gone mad, telling tales of spirits and of voices echoing in their heads"

Wait... What? Voices? Where had I heard that before?

I waved off her concern and continued. "When we reached the summit, she attacked me. Everything went black and when I regained consciousness, I was alone. It has taken me all this time to find her again."

Aoife frowned, "But she doesn't know you, at least, she acts like she has no knowledge of you,"

I shrugged. "Its... Complicated"

She nodded. "All well and good, so long as I know from which direction you're coming Jen, and so long as it's not the same direction as the hag then we will not find ourselves at cross purposes. Mayhap someday you can tell me the rest of the story."

I laughed sheepishly, "Am I so transparent?"

She reached over an pulled up the hood on my cloak, covering my hair from the rain. "To someone who has raised five children? Yes, you are, as you say, transparent, but we all have things we do not wish to share. Even me" The last was murmured so that I barely heard.

It took us another 2 hours to reach the market by which time the awkward silence had turned companionable and we set out to do battle with the merchants for their wares.

Chapter 10

It was about three weeks later, and I had just about finished with my morning 'lessons' with Bran when I heard the shouting, I opened my eyes and peered out the doorway, towards where the sound was coming from and could see Aoife standing in the middle of the track, barring the approach of two riders who were moving down the path towards her. That woman was gonna get herself hurt one of these days, I mean there were two riders...

Let me say that again. Two riders. On horses. Bearing down on her. And she just stood there, hands on her hips, denying them passage. I mean, they didn't look threatening, but things had a habit of going sideways and if you spent any length of time with me then you'd know it happened with annoying regularity. What was she thinking?? Assessing the situation as quick as I was able, I threw my cloak over my shoulders and stepped out into the light. My ears adjusted quicker than my eyes and I could hear a voice, two voices... Then I heard my name. A smile split my face as I started to jog across the field, and I approached the group at something close to a run.

It was Aed!! Glory be in the halls of the goddess, it was Aed. I hadn't realised quite how much I'd missed him but here he stood. Damn it was good to see him.

"Father told me where to find you and I came as soon as I was able. I'd have come sooner if my concern hadn't been calmed by the presence of the noble Balach," at this he winked at the boy, "and of course, there was the baby to consider."

I'm sorry what?? The Baby?? OMG!!! THE BABY!!!

The baby. The other rider threw back her hood and her hair blazed in the sun, of course it was Caoilin, and as soon as I'd finished wrestling Aed out of his saddle I turned to her.

"I think we can manage on our own" she laughed, I noticed the "we" almost immediately and after like a second it clicked. There, carried in a fold of her clothes, was the smallest, most perfect of children. Needless to say, as soon as Aoife realised it was Caoilin and that there was a baby in play she threw caution to the wind and descended upon us all like the rain in summer.

I introduced her. "The woman who is currently trying to steal your daughter away and secretly adopt her is Aoife, Balach's mother, though, it occurs to me that you've probably already met. Caoilin laughed and nodded. I continued, "Truth be told, if she hadn't been here to look after me these last few weeks, I'm pretty sure I'd have starved or died of sunburn or something. Don't let her formidable appearance fool you, I'm pretty sure anyone in need would find a welcome in her home."

Aed smiled "I can see from where Balach gets his good heart and his generous spirit."

I agreed. "Between the two of them I find that I want or need for nothing." With the introductions out of the way, the child commanded all of our attention and the women, myself included, contrived to spirit him away. The child, which, at this moment, was sitting on my knee, stared unblinkingly into my eyes. "What's her name?" I asked quietly.

"Well," said Caoilin "Aeds father told us of what you did for Balach, and we were wondering if you would bless us, bless our child, with a naming." I swear my head did a full-on exorcist twist, I was speechless... She rushed on "It's not just that it would be a huge honour for us personally, but as Aed pointed out, it would give your name a status that would be hard to ignore."

I looked at them. "Why do I get the feeling that there is more going on here than meets the eye?

"Aed smiled but it was Caoilin who answered, "Conlann..."

"My father" interjected Aed.

...has in recent months come to realise that his association with the Hag and her accomplice is perhaps a mistake. They have, over the last year, stripped him of most of his authority and now that he finally perceives their ill will he finds himself powerless to act. Without help, he can in no way see how to escape their domination. It is his hope, indeed his intention, that you become a lodestone to those people in the Glen disaffected with both his rule and with that false priestess who now holds sway."

Lord that girl could talk.

This was a lot to take in. "In return for your aid in freeing the Glen from the Hag's oppression he has vowed that he will stand aside in favour of Aed and take up a life of quiet contemplation. The objective now is peace. Peace and prosperity. A goal for which he would now sacrifice himself in order to secure it for the people, the Glen and for his family." She smiled at me, "Please say you will help us, you're really the only one who can."

I stood, feeling suddenly trapped by events. I could almost feel them reaching out to ensnare me. Bran had warned me of this, the longer you stay in a particular time and place the more you become a part of it and when the moment arrives, the harder it is to leave. Stay long enough and time sneaks back into your life to claim you and you begin to age again. For the first time, I could understand what he meant. These people, these places, these friendships all served to anchor me here. To this time and this place.

"I… I... Need to think… Please, make no more mention of this, we'll discuss it more tonight after dinner. You WILL stay for dinner, won't you??"

"Of course, they will" cried Aoife with a laugh,"the first people I've had the chance to actually talk to in weeks what with you being holed up in your sanctuary and Balach out and about doing whatever it is he does. They will stay for dinner and that's the end of it!"

I looked at Aed and laughed. "That's you telt."

******

Dinner was a quiet affair and talk quickly drifted to the matter at hand. "You realise you are essentially talking about revolution, don't you?" I asked the pair of them. "You are attempting to use my naming of your daughter, to create an alternative centre of power in the valley, someone to whom the people will turn to rather than the established order at

Dunadd. What exactly are you gonna do if Callie finds out about this before everything is in place? She will do everything she can to stop you. She will hunt you down and I have no doubt she will kill you. She will kill you both and she will kill your daughter. You don't know this woman like I do. There is nothing she won't do."

Caoilin looked confused, she looked at Aed, "Who is Callie?"

"I'm sorry," I interrupted before Aed could explain, "Callie is the Priestess. She and I have... History together."

There was a collective indrawing of breath, "You KNOW her???" Caoilin gasped.

I nodded, "It's complicated but yes, I have had experience of her before now." The silence dragged out until it felt obliged to fill it. "She was my friend. She was one of my only friends. That is, until she tried to kill me. Well, not kill exactly, more just tried to get me out of the way. I think her real problem is... Was... With my grandfather."

Aed nodded sadly, "Feuds are terrible things and oft times can result in the extinction of entire clans."

I nodded in agreement. Whatever else transpired, I think it was fair to say that what was going to happen between Callie and I, it most definitely wasn't going to involve flowers and rainbows. Just at that point the baby started to grumble so without thinking twice I picked the wee mite up, popped him over my shoulder and headed into the house, "I'll put him to bed, make yourselves at home. I'll be back in a minute."

I sat down on the bed and sat her on my knee, she had her mother's features but unlike Caoilin she had the most incredibly clear blue eyes, filled with trust and completely unclouded by the toil of day-to-day life to which she was doomed to follow. I stroked my hand down her face marvelling at the perfection when she reached up and took hold of my finger. And there we stayed, locked together, my heart more than my finger locked in her steely grip until her eyes closed and her breathing indicated she had fallen asleep. Disentangling myself from her grip I stood, more conflicted than ever, and stepped back out into the light of the fire…

******

Morning dawned. Well, I say dawned, but the sun was as sluggish as I this morning and the mist lay stretched across the valley like a blanket. Hugging the ground as only scotch mist can…

My mind, as filled with fog as the glen, refused to kick into gear so as per usual my feet took charge and without much effort found their way down to my sanctuary. I sat, crossed my legs, and took a deep cleansing breath. It was a trigger I'd created and conditioned my mind to obey. A couple of deep breaths and a sense of calm just dropped into my mind. My eyes were closed, and I could suddenly hear. The cows bellowing further down the glen needing milked, the rhythmic sound of someone hammering and the wind gently sighing in the trees, bringing messages from afar. I was connected to it all and I could feel it flowing into me and through me, renewing and revitalising me. Deep breath in… And sigh it out. I opened my eyes. I'd found that if I did this each morning and every night, my mind was clearer, and it was a lot easier to get in contact with my inner Bran. I sat, completely relaxed, probing the corners of my mind, waiting for his presence to resolve itself and all I could hear was the echo of my own heart beating the drum of my life. Whether it was a question to which there was no answer or whether he was deliberately

127

staying quiet was open to debate but for this moment at least, I was on my own.

It was a strange thing, to have Bran in my head. I mean, it wasn't exactly Bran, there were differences but over the last couple of weeks, I'd learnt a great deal about the history of this glen, the history of the Stones and the Circles and more importantly the knowledge of how to use them. I could return home whenever I wished and yet the knowledge had hooked me. As I'm sure Bran knew it would. What was it they said? With great knowledge comes great responsibility? Well, I felt a responsibility to this place and to these people. The fact that I felt that I owed something to Bran was irrelevant. Here I was and here I was gonna stay. Well, For the time being at least.

I took a last, deep breath and opened my eyes... Nothing. I had nothing. I guess I'd better start thinking of a name. And it had to be an appropriate name. Regardless of all other considerations, Aed and Caoilin were my friends and I always try and do right by my friends. Naming their daughter wasn't just any old responsibility. It was a BIG responsibility. I would, to all intents and purposes, be the child's Godmother.

I swear if a single one of you says ANYTHING about fairy godmothers I will travel to your time. I will find you. And, well, I'll be really grumpy at you.

Aed saw me first as I was returning over the fields and started towards me. He stopped me with a hand on my shoulder. "I'm sorry we dumped this on you, we should never have asked you like this. You must feel free to say no and I realise we didn't even give you that chance. A naming should never be done under duress, or the child will forever live under the shadow of obligation."

I looked at him. Really looked at him. There was no lie in his eyes or in his voice, just concern for me and for his people. How could I refuse such a request from such a good man? I smiled, "Yes."

I'm not sure he really understood what I'd said so I took his hand and said it again. "Yes. I would be honoured to name your child." The way his face lit up with joy and hope made it the right decision, regardless of the political consequences.

We decided to do it that evening, and Balach was sent hither and yon with a message to the people who lived close by. There was a naming in the offing and a party would be had. By the time Balach returned the sun was getting low in the sky and, not needing any excuse, a crowd had gathered from the local steadings. There was a bonfire blazing in the field and the whole thing had taken on the air of a celebration. It wasn't often there was a naming and even less often that the child was the defacto heir to the throne and the naming was to be done by a priestess.

Since it had turned into a bit of an event I'd decided to put on my cloak. Just to give it that air of solemnity you understand.

Not because I looked like someone out of any number of my favourite books. Honest. Seriously though, I wasn't above a bit of theatre when the occasion demanded it.

A hush fell over the crowd, and I looked up to see Aed and Caoilin, attended by Aoife and Balach, step out of the farmhouse, and walk across the field towards the fire. The sun was just starting to set and the whole glen was bathed in that glorious light; the gloaming. I was surrounded by friends, there was food and there was laughter. It was beautiful and for the first time in weeks I felt at home. It was one of those moments that stay etched in your mind for ever, and as always seemed to be the case with such moments, something inevitably comes along to spoil it.

That something, was Callie.

It started as a low murmuring from the back of the crowd, over by the gate, then raised voices... Shouting. You could feel the atmosphere of the crowd swirl and change. From happiness to fear. From fear, to anger. That amount of people gathered in the one place can create its own emotions, and emotions can change at the drop of a hat. They can be dangerous things.

In the very centre of the disturbance was a knot of men, a warband and riding at the very front was Callie, pushing her way through the crowd. She stopped not far away and looked down at me. Our eyes met and I held her gaze, projecting far more authority than I felt.

She smiled, as though she could see right through my bravado "Gwenhwyfief my dear, I'm distressed that you saw fit to arrange such a gathering without inviting me. Did my invite perhaps go astray? I missed your departure, You left our halls so quickly that I never had the chance to say goodbye."

I replied, oozing (fake) confidence. "There's absolutely nothing you can say that I need to hear, your presence here is neither wanted or needed, you are intruding on my land and upon my time. Turn around and leave this place."

She laughed, god, how I hated that laugh. "You speak as though you have some kind of authority here, I fear you have been sadly misinformed. You have no power beyond that which I choose to give you. You, are nothing." She gestured and a number of men split off from the close-knit group which surrounded her and pushed into the crowd. They grabbed hold of Aed and Balach, swords naked and, at least for the moment, unbloodied. Another grasped Caoilin by the hair, throwing her to the ground, tearing the baby from her grasp. I saw Aoife throwing herself at the man only to be pushed to the ground as well... Things were rapidly spiralling out of control.

I could feel the consciousness of the crowd swell and grow darker. It was like a wild dark thing straining against its bonds. All It'd take was a spark to ignite these smouldering embers and a raging inferno would engulf the entire valley. Callie had no idea of the danger she was in, that we were all in. If anything happened here, happened to the baby, then the rage which it would spawn would burst from this field and flood down the valley sweeping away any semblance of peace... People would die, houses would burn and Aed's father would be washed away in a tide of blood and fire, without ever having had the opportunity to make things right. The whole situation was balanced on a knife edge...

I shouted over the noise, "You know this isn't the time or place for this." I tried to place as much emphasis on the word time as I could, desperately trying to connect with her, trying to convey how I knew her, but it was useless. I could see in her eyes that she was riding the mood of the crowd like a champion surfer on a big wave. Feeling that power and mistaking it for her own. "Please..." I did the only thing I could think of and dropped to my knees, "Please... Just give me the child and GO". The cries of the baby soared out over the crowd like a wind fanning a brushfire. I literally felt it when she lost control, when the mob woke up and realised it was strong. She backed her horse up, suddenly aware that the mood had turned. That the anger was directed at her. One step... Another... Looking about for her men. Closer and closer to the fire she drew, her figure silhouetted against the flames.

I had a sudden moment of clarity. I could see what she was going to do. As clearly as if I were looking through a window into the future, "Wait... WAIT!!! "What are you doing!? Callie...stop!!!"

I realised too late what I'd said. At the mention of that name her eyes blazed. I could almost hear her mind snap as her temper broke." THAT'S. NOT. MY. NAME," she shrieked like a banshee. She wheeled her horse... Ranting... Matching the baby, scream for scream. Seizing her by the ankle she turned and, with a last, triumphant look, threw her into the fire.

******

Everything stopped. I could hear myself screaming... My mind blazing at what she had just done. The mood of the mob broke. I could feel the outrage, a dark seething thing looking for a weapon. A tool. Something it could use to lash out. To strike back.

It found me.

In that moment I could feel myself connected to the mob, connected to every person in the clearing, every person in the Glen. Conlann at Dunadd, Aoife, Balach, Aed, Caoilin, Callie, 'adad. I could feel them all; the presence of the stones, the circles, like a weight in my mind... My awareness stretched backwards in time to the very beginning and forward to the end - I could feel them all... Every one of them screaming with me at the outrage which had been committed on this night and for the first time, I felt the land, all that energy focused on one thing, focused through me, on the desire, the need, to make it all just STOP!

There was a blinding light. Every nerve in my body caught fire and I screamed in pain as my awareness was torn from my body. Even with my eyes closed, I could see, and I could hear. My mind encompassing everything but influencing nothing, Uselessly grasping at the strands of time which I had unknowingly torn asunder. I had become an observer to the unfolding of the paradox I had unwittingly created. I knew then. I had stopped something which had always been destined to occur but how could I not? How could I not try and save the baby? In that endless moment, broken beyond my ability to fix, time slowed. And stopped.

People and events frozen in time. Aed... Caoilin... Balach... All frozen mid struggle.

I could see and I could hear but I couldn't move. Was I doomed to be trapped in this frozen moment? Witnessing this abomination? Looking down from my disembodied vantage point, I could see myself. My body, standing in front of Callie, arms upraised, the nexus of an incredible maelstrom of forces that I couldn't hope to understand. Focussed on me. Infusing me. The baby, frozen in mid-air hanging suspended in the flames, motionless. Unmoving and untouched by the fury of the fire.

I struggled but it was in vain. The energy of the mob, of the stones, of the very land itself poured into me. I was being consumed and no matter what I did or what I tried; I couldn't let it go. I was going to die. Stuck frozen in this endless instant as the paradox consumed me. Bran had said it. He had warned me. Time must happen as it has happened, and I was going to be sacrificed to ensure that the river continued to flow.

I was helpless to save my friends. Helpless to save the baby. Then, echoing through the night and in my mind was a sound. If the whole of creation was an echo, then this was the sound of the bell which had produced it. It shook my soul and scraped on every nerve. I saw a point of light appear, glowing, spinning, brighter and brighter. Round and round, tracing golden spirals in the sky. Faster and faster, they spun joining and growing until there was a vast tearing sound and from out of nothing, as though slipping out from between the seconds stepped Bran.

He walked over to Callie. "I thought you could be turned from this path. At the very least I thought I could dissuade you from your constant meddling, but I fear this time you have gone too far, by this action you have damned yourself, cursed yourself throughout all of time. This act will follow you, will follow you wherever you go, indeed, I fear it will most likely be the end of you. He lifted his hand, suddenly blazing with light and touched it to her face. Even in this frozen moment I could feel her mind screaming... Crying out in pain as whatever Bran was doing seared into her very soul. Frozen in that endless moment I could only watch as he walked to the fire, reached into the flames, and pulled out the child. Unharmed as far as I could see. That done he turned and stared right at me, at my disembodied consciousness, I could see him reaching out, taking the torn threads of the timeline from my hands, and seamlessly knit them back together. He finished and with a flourish he threw them into the air.

I could feel the timeline reforming, the river suddenly flowing again. Diverted down a new path but flowing. Time moving forward once more.

What had I done?

More to the point, I think, is HOW had I done it?

I'd somehow manage to do the very thing which Bran had said was impossible for me to do and even worse than that, I had no idea how I'd done it.

Things were subtly suddenly different. I don't know what and I couldn't see when, but things had most definitely changed. Time had changed. I could feel it. Every part of me could feel it. He looked back at me, an eyebrow lifted quizzically. "I think it's about time you came back. Don't you?"

With a bone jarring thump, I felt myself back in my body, sight returning to my eyes, sound filling my ears... There was screaming and shouting as time lurched into its new course and there on her knees in front of me, was Callie. Screaming, tearing at her hair. Clawing at her face. All shreds of sanity vanished from her eyes... Aed and Balach had freed themselves in the confusion, and were advancing upon her, weapons drawn.

"Stop!!!" I shouted, "Let them go. Let her go" I said, half to myself. Her men, fear filling their eyes, gathered her up and executed what would later be described as a tactical retreat.

Bran walked over to Caoilin and offered her his hand. Taking it, she allowed him to pull her to her feet and to put his arm around her shoulders. He turned to the people. The farmers, the travellers, the bondsmen, all who had gathered. He held the child close and kissed her forehead and in a voice which I struggled to hear yet which I swear coulda been heard in Glasgow he murmured, "Through Jens actions you have been saved from death and have been born again from the flames, In honour of this I name you Eithne." With that he gently handed her to Caoilin. "Try not to lose her again, yes?"

There was absolute silence as he walked over to me. He stood before me, searching my face with his eyes. "Are you ok?" I nodded, mutely. "Are you sure?" Again, I nodded. "I'm sorry, I had no idea that you would have such a strong connection to this place..." His voice tailed off and he shook his head in consternation. "There are things I now need to fix, things that have been changed, disrupted by your actions here. The gods alone know what the consequences will be. Try and stay out of trouble until I get back or at least for the next wee while, yes??" I nodded again.

135

Apparently, my trip out into the aether had completely robbed me of the ability to talk. If I kept nodding like one of those dogs on the back shelf of a car no one was ever gonna take me seriously.

He stared at me for a second longer, touched my cheek gently and stepped away. He looked around at the assembled people, nodding to some, waving to others and finally returned his gaze to me. He lifted his hand and with a finger, trailing golden light, he drew a spiral in the air, stepped forward, and vanished.

Chapter 11

<u>Kilmartin. The Present Day. The Morning After.</u>

I stared at the face in the mirror, the colourless eyes staring back. My white hair and pale skin looking even worse than usual in the harsh glow of the bathroom light. I shook my head, trying to dislodge the thoughts which were crowding in on me, trying to get my attention. The events of yesterday morning pretty much top of the pile. Damnit Jen! Why couldn't you just have let well enough alone? Why did you have to be so like him?

Him. Maelgwyn.

My friend. My brother.

MINE!

Almost our whole lives it had been just us. Maelgwyn and I. From those early days on Anglesey, through the lost years in Branwens cottage and the horror of the time spent running and hiding from the accursed Romans. We'd been friends before.

We had...!!

Sometimes I'm not sure who I was trying to kid. In those early days we'd never been friends. He was a means to an end. I would have dropped him in a second if I'd thought it would have gotten me one step closer to that stone. But he always had something that I needed. Something that would bring us that little bit closer to our goal. A snippet of information. A rumour heard in the market. Something that kept him by my side.

Sometimes I wonder if he knew.

Of course, he knew, he probably knew me better than I ever knew myself.

Regardless. Friends or not. The terror of the fire, Branwen, all the running and hiding... All those experiences had served to just push us closer together, had made us family. In every sense of the word. There were days when I couldn't stand to even look at him. Days when his calm indifference to me made me want to scream. But the fact remained. It was just the two of us. We were all that was left of our people. All that was left of our village. Everyone we'd ever known had been washed away in a flood of blood and fire.

Ok. Yes, I admit that some of that had been entirely my fault, but she totally deserved it. They all did. Inevitably, that kind of thing will forge a bond between those who live through it. A bond which I thought would never, could never be broken. That day when we'd sworn the vow, to make them pay, well... That wasn't the one we'd sworn. That was the one I'd sworn, in the silence of my heart. The vow I'd sworn with Maelgwyn was to go back and save them but saving them didn't interest me.

Saving them didn't get me what I wanted. Saving them didn't get me taught by her. Saving them didn't bring me, 2000 years ago, to this very glen.

It had been such a simple plan. Come here. Worm our way into the confidence of the ruling elite. Use them to find what we wanted. Simple.

Not simple.

This place was a trap. This god forsaken glen. No matter how often I leave I always seem to be drawn back here. I'd lived here in various guises many times over the years. Every cursed stone, every carving, every tomb was as familiar as the scars on my arm. As much as anywhere, this place had become my home. No not my home. My prison.

It was right here that it all went so badly wrong. When everything just fell apart.

Everything.

But I'd make them pay. Every single one of them for what they had done. To me. To us. They would all pay.

I can't believe he could just walk away from that! I can't believe he could walk away from me... ME.!!! I saved him. His life belonged to ME. How could he just leave!!! God damnit!!! I smashed my hand down on the sink. Only Maelgwyn could get me this angry. Even after all this time.

Ok Callie. Deep breaths. Calm. Relax.

For the love of the goddess!!! How can I possibly relax with this god damned headache!!!

It was definitely a bad idea to come back here. I'm not even sure what had prompted it this time. There were just way way too many memories. Of all the places I could have gone, of all the different times... The trail always led back here. God damnit. Where were those painkillers!!

Please God let there be some in the cupboard, I couldn't even contemplate going outside on a day like this. It was starting to feel as though the sun would split my head right open. Even from in here, the light shining in the window was already beating itself on my exposed face. Things to do today flashed through my mind. There was so much I needed to do if I was going to leave today (tomorrow at the latest).

Damnit.

The only way I was going to accomplish even half of what I needed to get done (and even remember the other half) was to write a list.

I hated lists but there was no point in fighting the inevitable.

First off, I was going to have to leave. But where to go, or more to the point, when to go. I needed to get some stuff and I absolutely needed to get that knife. That stone knife. Something had happened. Sometime in the past. That knife was most definitely NOT in the stone last year. Someone had put it there. No. Not someone.

Him.

He'd put it there. Him or... or that other one. I could feel the goose bumps run right up my spine. If he'd decided to take a direct hand in events, then that was bad news. Really really bad news. Up until now we'd done nothing but irritate him but if he'd suddenly started directly interfering then someone somewhere must have REALLY pissed him off. He was everywhere. Every time. Hell, if I looked hard enough right now. Here. In this time. I could probably find him, hell if I meddled enough, he'd probably come find me. Whatever it was that he was calling himself these days. It wasn't the first time I'd had to leave sometime really quickly. Like that time when we started the rebellion right here and overthrew the chief.

God! If those I didn't find those painkillers soon, I was really gonna lose it...

That was the first time, the first time we'd tried to really change things. When we'd killed that whole family. Killed the baby. That was what had started it all. The fire. The screams. I still don't know why, what came over me.

But... Wait

I didn't kill the baby, did I??? That wasn't what happened. Not what I remember. But it was... I could distinctly remember... It... Taking the child because she was there. I wanted to hurt her. I wanted to hurt her as much as she had hurt me

Wait... What? Who???

Oh god my head... Its splitting... I feel like it's being torn in two...

Taking the child from her mother and throwing it in the fire. Burning... Burning... The screams... My screams...

Oh my god, what did you do...!!! What have you done to me...!!!???

What. Happened. I can't remember what happened. It's. All. Changed. Changing.

How is that possible. It's not possible. You can't change time. Not without...

The Stone!!!!!

Time has been changed!!!

I needed to go back. I needed to find out what had been changed. More to the point, I needed to find out HOW.

God, I hoped the circles were charged enough after yesterday. If I don't get a move on, then the questions about Jen would inevitably lead back to me. That could prove to be... Unfortunate.

For them.

What was it gonna take to get rid of the headache!!!!

Sod it.

It was just going to have to wait. I had stuff that needed to be done. I had a list.

The pain... What pain? It had stopped... Hadn't it??

Book 2

Chapter 12

The sound of laughter woke me. Laughter and the smell of burnt toast. Now, I'm not gonna say that this was the normal state of affairs, but it happened often enough that it felt, or should I say smelt, like home. I lay there, my mind travelling back to the night before, remembering the terrible screaming. The look of utter nothing in Callie's eyes. I have no idea what Bran had done, but would you believe I was almost starting to feel sorry for her? Yeah, I know, I'm way too soft hearted but seriously, if you've ever seen, and I mean that literally, somebodies mind break into tiny little pieces then you'd feel sorry for them too.

Not wanting to let such sombre thoughts ruin the day I dragged my aching body out of bed. Dear god but I was sore. I felt like I had just completed the local pre-roman triathlon. Literally every bone in my body hurt.

I learnt later that my battered body was a result of the unceremonious way in which my consciousness slammed back into my body the night before. Apparently, there are right and wrong ways to do this.

Who knew??

Right. I can do this. I can. Clothes being the first order of the day. As awesome as Balach is and as much as he had become the little brother that I'd never had, the last thing I wanted to do was mentally scar us both by stumbling from bed half naked looking for a drink of water. We were close. But not that close.

Check me out, fully dressed and not a single thing put on backwards or inside out. I should get an award. Girl dresses self! Woop!!! Seriously though. You should try living in a culture which hasn't discovered the button yet. Or the zipper. It's not as easy as you think.

Time travel movies never seem to cover that. The devil is in the details 'adad always used to say and boy was he right.

The other week I'd had to ask Aoife for help getting dressed and you've no idea how embarrassing that was to a 15-year-old girl. Yeah, Hi could you show me how to fasten my top??

Not humiliating at all.

From that point on she just treated me like a child although, she had definitely relaxed that of late. I guess she had finally come to the point where she was satisfied that I might just be able to look after myself after all.

Finally, fully dressed and almost presentable I braced myself for the inevitable burnt toast and stepped out into the kitchen come living area of the house.

There, sitting at the table, was Bran.

I honestly don't know why I was surprised. The way he just showed up unannounced and left with no notice was becoming almost predictable. Just here one moment, gone the next. I mean don't get me wrong, I was really glad to see him, I had questions and more questions and there was a fair chance (If I could actually get him to talk) that he had answers, but it was still frustrating as hell.

He looked at me in silence, but I swear I could hear him laughing. "What?? No semi nakedness and begging for water? I'm disappointed. Here was me thinking we were about to be treated to the great priestess lowering herself to talk with us mere mortals." I stuck my tongue out at him and moved to block the escape route should breakfast decide to make a break for it. It was just toasted bread, but it paid to be sure. Just in case. I wrestled a couple of slices onto what passed for a plate and doused it in fresh butter. Bran opened his mouth to speak again but I held up one finger and shushed him before he got started. Priorities people! Food first. Talk later.

Oh god that was sooo much better. The headache which had been threatening since I got up withered and died under the assault of so many carbs and I finally resigned myself to the scolding which I was sure Bran was about to give me. I could put it off no longer. I glanced up at him. Sitting there, eyebrow raised. Looking for all the world like a normal, everyday human being and reluctantly gave him the go-ahead to continue.

"A good morning to you too, your holiness," Bran announced, sarcasm dripping from his every word, I smiled in spite of myself. "That was quite some party you threw last night. Is there anything else you'd like to do? Divert the river? Maybe knock down some stones? Why not just change the seasons whilst you're at it? I can't wait to see what else you've got planned. Though maybe give me a bit of warning next time, my nerves aren't quite what they were and I'm not sure I can take any more of these surprises."

"Ha!!!!"

I'm sorry, I just couldn't keep that one in.

"God, you're one to talk. You appear from literally nowhere and I mean nowhere. You weren't hiding. You weren't in the crowd. I saw you! You literally stepped out of nowhere. You rescue the baby, curse a woman. That was a curse, wasn't it? I didn't imagine what I saw, did I? (not that she didn't deserve to be cursed. She totally did) and then, once everything was sorted, you up sticks and bugger off back to wherever it is you go to when you're not here pestering me!"

I meant to say all that. I did. I meant every single word too. What I didn't mean to happen was the milk that came snorting out of Brans nose when I said the word bugger and the coughing and spluttering that ensued.

"Speaking of Callie... She WILL recover right? I mean the Callie I knew and loved from back home was absolutely perfectly sane. A little wacked out yeah, but still completely sane."

He looked a little shifty when he replied, "Yes... She will recover. Eventually. I'm not sure how, or why... But she will recover. The curse however will follow her to the end of her days. Indeed, it will most likely be the end of her days."

I shuddered. Not particularly enjoying the direction of the conversation. I turned to Aed who until then had been sitting at the table looking like he was sharing breakfast with a live snake. Desperately trying to appear nonchalant but his eyes were a little wide round the edges.

147

"I don't believe I've had the chance to introduce you, have I?" I asked them. "Aed... This is Bran, my teacher," and because I was feeling particularly inclusive... "And my uncle" The extended fit of choking he launched into made it totally worthwhile. "Bran? This is Aed. My friend and my guide from the moment I landed here. In the Glen I mean." Looking at Aed, from under my lashes, hoping against hope that he hadn't noticed my almost slip of the tongue. "Now shake hands and make nice whilst I make myself some tea and, whilst I'm at it if you could make yourself useful and turn the spit. Aoife will have all of our asses if we let this burn and don't think I haven't noticed how neither of you were paying the slightest bit of attention."

I poured the hot water into a cup and looked in askance at Bran. "Tea?" He shrugged and I poured another cup. The Dandelions I had been collecting and drying, when sweetened with a spoonful of honey actually made a passable cup of tea. Don't get me wrong. Right now, I would kill for a large cappuccino, but needs must I suppose.

Bran stared into his cup before taking a sip. He shook his head and, I'm pretty sure rolled his eyes as well. "I'm not even going to comment."

"What???"

"Does the concept of not interfering in things actually mean anything to you? I'm guessing not and quite frankly, after your antics last night, inventing Dandelion tea is a small thing.

What? Did he think I was gonna drink nothing but water the whole time I was here? Nuh uh. Think again pal. A girl needs her morning... uh... Coffee substitute.

"Right. Now that we have that out of the way, why don't you tell me what is going on." I glanced at Bran, "I don't imagine you just popped by 'cause you were in the local... area."

He looked amused at my poor attempt at humour, "I wasn't anywhere near the area, truth be told but I did, as you say, pop in, just to make sure you were ok. That was an unbelievable accumulation of power that you focussed last night Jen. Such things very rarely ever happen without consequences. For you, for those involved, for the very fabric of reality."

Aed dropped his cup.

"Goddess save me Bran. You can't just waltz in here, drop some fabric of reality hoo-hah and expect the natives to just smile and nod. It's not normal!!" He sighed. "Fine." He looked at Aed. "I take it you understand that I'm not from around here?" Aed mutely nodded. "Ok, let's just go with that. I'm not from here and I'm Jen's teacher."

"Her teacher" said Aed, "Not her uncle?" Bran looked at me, a mischievous twinkle in his eye. "Almost. But not quite"

Ok... I admit... This time it was me who dropped the cup.

"What?? How??" Would you believe the smug git actually winked at me? "What do you mean Almost???"

He laughed. "Calm down Jen... I was kidding. Kind of. No, I was. I was kidding!" He ducked as I threw the bread at him.

Kidding??? He was kidding??? This is not a ha ha moment for me buster.

I took a deep breath. "God you are so infuriating!!"

Would you believe he actually had to nerve to look contrite? "I apologise. I came at, what I assumed, to be your need. I was carving and felt reality shudder. That's as best I can describe it and I just knew it had something to do with you. I jumped, quite wrongly, to the conclusion that you were in need and so I came. Imagine my surprise to find that you had the whole thing well in hand. Indeed, that help against the Hag was the last thing that you needed. He sighed then, fidgeting in his chair. Why don't we just start at the beginning. You tell me what it is that you actually remember, and I will do my best to fill in any gaps."

Staring down at the table I cast my mind back, letting the memories from last night rise to the surface. "I don't know, everything was completely normal. Horrible, but normal. Callie arrived with her men. Aed and Balach were being held and Callie had the baby. I... I said something..."

"What? What did you say Jen?"

"It was her name. I said her name and she just lost it. I know it's not her name in the here and now but even by her standards this was an overreaction. She just went crazy and threw Eithne into the fire!!" I paused…

"What happened then?" He asked gently…

"I... I don't know. It was as if there was all this energy just flowing into me from everywhere. I felt so strong, like I could do anything, and it just kept building and building. I knew exactly what it wanted me to do, could feel what it needed me to do but I had no idea how to do it. It just kept building. More and more power. I felt like an over inflated balloon. Like my very skin was stretched taught across my entire body and I still had no way to release it. No way on knowing how."

I was sounding a little hysterical even to my own ears.

"Then something inside me broke. It was if a barrier or something just dissolved. That was when everything thing just kind of burst out of me..."

Aed had taken my hand and was holding it tight, holding me together. I had my eyes shut, trying to remember. Trying to relive last night. "Every fibre of my being was focussed on saving the baby. I couldn't let her die. I was her godmother. It was my duty to protect her. The baby would not, could not die. Every fibre of my being willed that outcome but there was no way I could have reached them in time. No way I could stop what was going to happen. I can remember desperately trying to reach out with my mind. Willing it. Wishing it?"

He frowned at that, "Wishing?"

I shook my head. "Wishing? Praying? All I know is I was trying to reach them. Trying to stop Callie. Trying to catch the baby." I suddenly understood. That was when it all went pear shaped. I'd provided all that power with a direction. A purpose. "There was an enormous flash of light as it surged from my mind and an incredible surge. Suddenly, somehow, I was no longer in my body. I could see and I could hear but... I don't know... It's getting harder and harder to explain, details keep slipping away from me, I just... I don't know what happened. I don't know how I did it. I don't even know if it WAS me who did it. I just don't know!!"

Aed squeezed my hand. "Well, if it helps, the villagers are in absolutely no doubt about what happened. You saved Eithne, Jen. You called down the wrath of the gods on the priestess's head and in the same breath a blessing on my girl. You ARE the High Priestess in their minds and nothing you say is going to change that."

I groaned. That was all I needed. Word spreading up and down the glen that I was some sort of all powerful voodoo woman with the gods on speed dial and a pocket full of thunderbolts. "Listen Aed, I know this is all in keeping with your grand plan but what's going to happen when all these people show up at my door demanding miracles and all I can provide is burnt toast and the occasional bad joke?"

Bran chimed in "Jen's right, from what she has said it's apparent that she had no real control over what happened last night. That could prove to be dangerous should certain parties take issue with how events last night turned out. If either of you are going to make capital out of this then you're going to have to move quickly. Callie may be temporarily out of the picture but let's not forget that she is not the only issue. She has allies. She didn't arrive in the Glen by herself she came with the Bodach and that alone should give us pause."

Aed continued with the whole rabbit in headlights thing he had going on. "Her companion? I'm not sure I know what his name is, but I've certainly never heard him called that. What is it? Some kind of title? He's not even that old."

Bodach is Gaelic for old man. My apologies, I keep forgetting not all of us are blessed with a magical aptitude for languages.

"Well, if he's not calling himself that, what IS he calling himself these days?" Asked Bran. Aed shrugged, "I'm not entirely sure I've ever heard him referred to as anything. He is always just kind of there, in the background. I'm not trying to say that she is the brains and that he is the brawn, but he really doesn't talk much, and he IS kind of threatening."

"His name is Maelgwyn."

At the sound of a new voice, I turned to find Aoife in the doorway.

"His name is Maelgwyn," she repeated, "and he and that hag are Prytani, come here from Ynys Mon, an island betwixt Prydein and Ierne."

I was literally gobsmacked... "How, do you know this??" I stuttered.

More to the point, how did I not even know my own granddads name. Or the fact that he was WELSH?!

"When they arrived, we were still engaged in that tit for tat conflict with the men of the Hen Ogledd. Balachs father had been gone for going on seven years and still it dragged on, taking the lives of the people. All of this just served to make it easier for them when they arrived." She paused. Her eyes far away, "He was happier back then, different to what he has become, and we became friends. More than friends. But then one day..." She paused, "I don't know, something happened." She laughed, bitterly. "I say something, but I know exactly what happened. It was her. I know it was her. She was enraged at the thought that he could possibly have a relationship with anyone but her. Words were spoken, threats were made. At the time I had no way of fighting for what I wanted and... Well, she has some, I don't know, some kind of hold over him, I know not what, but from then on, he wouldn't talk, wouldn't even look at me. Eventually, though it pained me, I just stopped trying."

I hugged her. What else could I do? She seemed so sad. Aed cleared his throat, almost apologetically. "A thought occurs..."

Great. Now even Aed was starting to sound like Bran. I swear that man should not be allowed to mix with polite company.

"...Maybe now, with the priestess out of the way, indisposed as it were, then the good Aoife can talk to him, reason with him, maybe even persuade him to take the hag and leave this place. For good."

Wouldn't it be easier, and more permanent to just kill her?" Aoife looked at us all. "Don't say you weren't all thinking it. It is by far the simplest solution and the most likely to produce a permanent solution. I'm sure we don't want her coming back and taking back what she considers to be hers."

"We can't kill her." Bran's statement was blunt.

"Of course we can." She replied. "A sharp knife. A heavy club. It's pretty easy to kill someone my lord Bran. You just need a little bit of planning and some patience."

He shook his head again. More emphatically this time, in the face of Aoife's brutally simple solution. "We can't. I say that in the strongest possible terms. We simply can't kill her. It would cause too much of a disruption to, well, to everything. I think our best bet is to go with Aeds plan. If we can gain access to Maelgwyn then hopefully Aoife can talk to him. Persuade them to leave."

I sat and thought about it and the more I thought about it the more I realised that it was a good idea. Not just good but quite brilliant. If we could accomplish our goals without bloodshed, then so much the better.

Once again it was Bran who struck a discordant note. "I hate to spoil the party and all that, but you may want to consider taking a couple of people with you when you go, say 40 or 50 people. It might even be an idea to arm them. Just in case things go pear shaped as you say in your world. Just because Callie is no longer holding the reins doesn't mean he will want to speak to you. He might not WANT to go. There are things that can be done. Spells that can be used that will tie a person to you. Bind them to you, body, and soul. Just because Callie is no longer about doesn't necessarily mean she isn't still in control. Having some sort of plan B might not be a bad idea."

Ok, great, important safety tip there from Bran. Safety first. Walk quietly but carry a really big pointy stick. Made of metal. And sharp on both sides. So… Walk quietly and carry a sword. A big sword. Ok. You get the picture. Be Careful!! seemed to be the order of the day.

Let's be honest, there isn't a single person in that room who actually wanted to get within a field's length of that mad woman without a wall of armed people separating them.

"Aed!" I snapped my fingers, "Earth calling, Aed. Come on Aed, focus, how quickly can you gather that many men?"

"Is it just men that you'll be wanting with you on this expedition? Not all of us are like the gentle Aoife…"

She obviously missed the bit of the conversation where Aoife went all Warrior Princess on us.

"…there are many women. Wives and mothers both that would be wanting to have a word with that hag themselves." Caoilin had decided to enter the fray and for the first time I noticed that she also wore a sword. Now I'm no shrinking violet, being a child of the noughties and all that but this was Game of Thrones levels of badassery. It was a definite look.

"Jeeze, Caoilin you just need some horns on your helmet and you're good to go," I joked.

She looked at me, completely deadpan "I don't think that'd be a good idea, they'd snag on every overhanging branch and give your enemy something to grab and pull your head down."

I sighed. Obviously, my rapier wit was wasted on these people. Salvaging what was left of my dignity I set them to moving. "Right, we need at least 40, at most 50, armed and if possible armoured people to meet with us here, tomorrow morning at noon. I'm thinking it's long past time we finished this."

Chapter 13

I could easily jump ahead now to the big confrontation and all that, but real life isn't like that. Things have to be arranged. People have to gather. Horses need saddled. And in between times, life continues to happen. Sometimes in ways not even Bran could foresee.

The following morning dawned cold and damp. Aoife was already up when I finally dragged myself from bed. She and Balach were deep in conversation, well, I say conversation... What I mean is that Balach stood and listened, whilst Aoife talked. "Go to Gabran in the next glen and Loarn as well. This is as much their problem as it is ours and they'd be upset if we failed to invite them," Balach nodded, "and you brothers. See if you can't find them. Last I heard, Oengus was living with the widow up by the fairy mounds. He should know where the rest can be found. We can trust them to..." She caught sight of me... "Do as they are told. Good morning your holiness..."

I was getting a little bit tired of all this your holiness this. Your holiness that and coupled with everything that was going on I could perhaps be forgiven for being just a little bit grumpy. I grabbed myself a cup of tea and indicated I was going down to the sanctuary to do some thinking.

Maybe a little bit of sleeping. Hey, you never know. Thinking can be exhausting.

There was so much going on that I hadn't really had time to come to terms with everything that was happening. I had so many questions that I needed an answer to and yet I knew that no answers would be forthcoming.

I stood and stared at it. It was just the oddest little building. This and my cottage were anomalies. Buildings out of time, and yet nobody had been able to explain to me how they came to be here. Still, it offered me a place to escape the outside world. I called it my sanctuary and in truth it really had become that. It was cool, it was dry, and a feeling of calm pervaded the entire structure. Not only that but it was completely private. For whatever reason, superstition, or courtesy or whatever, no one had the nerve to bother me in here. The moment I stepped inside it was like stepping into a blessed cool shower. I let out a deep sigh of relief.

I nearly leapt out of my skin when a voice from the darkness said. "I think it's time that we started being honest with each other. Don't you?"

Even though I couldn't see him, I recognised the voice as Bran. Though… Bran with an edge to his voice.

"There was absolutely no way you should have been able to do what you did last night Jen. You are the granddaughter of a trained Druid, someone who used the circles extensively. That in itself will have changed you but apart from maybe the occasional oddity, dreams, and such things, it shouldn't have changed you to the extent that you could do what you did last night."

"You need to understand Jen. What you did, he paused, shaking his head in bewilderment, "do you even know what you did? Aed and Caoilin's baby died. I can remember it. I lived it. It kindled a fire which swept down this valley and ended up with Aeds father dead and him installed as king. Callie and Maelgwyn fled before the flames, leaving the king to his fate and their plan in ruins. With your single action, you've changed time. I have no idea what's going to happen next." He shook his head again... "She died. You've changed time Jen and that should be... Never mind should... BY any standard it IS impossible. There were those amongst my own kind who could, with enough training, alter small things... But you... What you did was huge! You changed someone from being dead. To alive! That changes everything. Knowing what you know and with what little experience you have there is no way you should have ever been able to do that."

He stepped forward into the light and the look on his face and the tone of his voice gave me pause. "Now, bearing that in mind, the question remains... Who, exactly, are you?"

He was on a roll now, The words spilling from his mouth, talking to himself as much (if not more) than at me. "Did they send you? Was it Ogma? Nuada? I can tell you right now that I won't go back. I've been here, doing the duty that they abandoned, for thousands of years. I won't go back. There is nothing you can do to force that. They can sit and wither in their underground cities for all that I care. I will keep the world on its course, the way that Danu taught us, the way the Dagda commanded us."

Wow... Turns out you CAN learn stuff if you keep your mouth shut...

"Uh... I have no idea what it is that you're talking about. Who are these people? Ogma?? Nuada?? And where is it exactly that they want you to return to?"

Bran looked at me in absolute horror. "You mean you're not...?" His voice trailed off... "Then who ARE you???"

"I don't understand what you mean" I sounded freaked out even to my own ears, "What do you mean 'who am I??' It's me! Jen... I'm the same Jen that I've always been."

"Jen... what you did last night... I can't even begin to explain how far out of your reach that should have been. There are beings and creatures out there who could maybe, at a push, do what you did last night but believe me when I say, humanity isn't one of them. It should have snuffed your mind and consciousness out like a candle and that's before tearing your body apart atom by atom. There's a reason you don't mess with time. Even my people only ever did it in small ways and then only after long preparation and if they had no other choice. No human could have survived. You should quite literally be dead. More than that. You should no longer exist."

I just stood and stared at him in shock.

"The obvious answer would appear to be that you are not entirely human. That somewhere in your ancestry is someone, or something, that rides with the wild hunt."

This was getting a bit much, even for me. "Rides with the what?"

"Never mind. Forget I said anything." He seemed ready to calm back up, but I had the bit between my teeth now and I wasn't going to let this go. He had said too much. Hinted at too much. I wanted answers and I wanted them now. I was tired of being moved around like a piece on some kind of giant chess board.

"Can't you tell??? I demanded. "I mean, you could do that thing that you did back when first we met. Back when I couldn't explain how I'd come to be there... Can't you look into my mind and see??

He shook his head, "It's not that simple... That was a relatively small thing. All that involved was the unspooling of your memories to see what you remembered. It looks impressive but it's really just a quicker way of my getting the answers I needed without the laborious task of actually talking to you."

Laborious? Really? Had he listened to himself recently?

What your asking is something else completely. You're asking me to delve into your genetic memory. To go back and see the reality of who you are as opposed to the fiction that most people live with, who you *think* you are. That's a different proposition entirely and can cause irreparable damage to the psyche. You could lose yourself amongst all the other personalities submerged in your genetic make-up... Even if you manage to survive undamaged it's unlikely you would survive unchanged. Some people are driven mad by true self-awareness."

He made to leave, but I grabbed his arm and turned him back to face me. "From everything that you've seen, from everything that you've learnt about me, do I seem to be the type of person who would break? Do I look like the kind of person who is going to let this go?"

He sighed. "Just forget I said anything."

"No!!!! Damnit Bran. It was you who said we had to be honest with each other. That cuts both ways! I have literally told you everything I know and anything I haven't told you; you've leached directly from my mind. You quite probably

161

know more about me than I know about myself. I know absolutely nothing about you. Who you are, where you come from? What your stake is, in all of this...?? You can tell me these things Bran. You can trust me. It's not like I'm going to tell anybody. Hell, it's not like I have anyone to tell!! I haven't freaked out yet, though if you don't start talking then I'm gonna start doing things my way." I was shouting now. "You've shown me how to use the circles, you've hinted at how to use the stones. Start talking or I might start experimenting. Hell, I might just decide to go home, and you can all be damned."

Emotional much?

The silence stretched out between us... It was one of those moments that could make or break a friendship and we both knew it. Finally, he reached out and offered me his hand. "I will tell you what I can. Be aware though, there are things that I won't tell you and there are things that I can't, but in those instances, it is for your, and in some cases, my own safety. Will that satisfy you?"

I started to object "But..." He cut me off... "I am already dancing dangerously close to a line that I dare not cross Jen, don't push it."

I looked at him, standing there with his hand outstretched and for the first time there was no twinkle in the eye, there was no one sided smile. For the first time since I'd met him, he looked serious. Proper serious. I took his hand, "I'm sorry Bran, I'll accept whatever it is that you feel able to tell me. I apologise for pushing, it has been a mad couple of days. Friends??"

He smiled and nodded, "Friends, although maybe you should perhaps wait until after you have heard my tale. Friendship is not such a little thing after all."

Circles and Stones

I know it's a bit of a cliché, but it really did feel like the sun had come out from behind a cloud.

Sunshine. But with a chill in the wind.

I shivered, trying to see his face in the darkness. "Do you, uh, want to go for a walk?"

In response he gestured at the door. I stepped out, the sunlight momentarily blinding me. "You're right," he said. "Some things are, most definitely, better spoken about in the light of the sun." "Come." And he set off across the fields, heading towards the Temple Wood where first I'd met him all those years ago.

Well… I say years… It was actually no more than a couple of months, but it was really starting to feel like I'd known him for sooo much longer than that. This whole time travelling thing was really starting to do my head in.

We walked in silence until I was seriously starting to think he'd forgotten I was there. We stood outside the old stone circle. The place where it had all started. The crow, who had become my shadow, settled into the branches of a tree and its call echoed in my mind. Bran glanced at it and sat down, shaking his head slightly. I was about to say something when he motioned me to sit and without waiting, started talking…

"My people are old Jen… We were old before the walls of Ilium fell, old before Imhotep and the Aegyptians learned how to build mountains in the desert. Before the Minoans sailed the inner seas. We were here before them all and in those days of happiness we lived in four great cities. Cities of art and light and laughter. Falias it was that was builded in the south, Gorias we caused to be raised in the west, Murias crowned an island in the East and Finias, my own beloved city of lights, our home from ages past, was built in the north."

163

His story had caught me and worlds, un-dreamt of, were spun out of my imagination by the power of his words. "From these four cities we lived and laughed and spread our light amongst the tribes of man for such was our task. To guide. To Teach. In sharp prowed ships of glass we sailed the seas, from the farthest north, where the lands are locked 'neath rivers of Ice and skies burn with astral fire, to the deepest south where the sun has scorched the land and water becomes a luxury. We sailed the seas and we spread our wisdom. Mountains of stone we raised wherever we went, and the world blossomed under our care. This was before the dark times. Before the pride of my people brought down upon us the anger of the goddess."

The crow which had, until that moment been perched on one of the stones chose that moment to throw itself into the air. The harshness of its call echoing back down to us Bran shook his head and continued.

"In fire and water, she laid waste to our land. Pestilence and famine she inflicted upon the Land of Glass. With rains of fire, she devastated the Isle of Apples. A wave of blood and darkness overwhelmed the high walls of Falias, and the curse of mortality left the gilded halls of Gorias empty, echoing no more with the laughter of children but with lamentation and tears. Across the land and seas, we fled. Our leaders and near all of our people fell to the darkness so that barely one in ten survived. Our brightest and strongest, Brave Leyr. Skilled Goibniu and Wild Cernunnos all made the ultimate sacrifice in defence of our retreat. Sadly diminished we survived and in bare nine ships, we fled that final shore. Nine times nine days we sailed. Nine times nine lands we passed over until, bereft of hope, and desperate for home, we arrived in Ierne bearing before us the treasures of our people."

Ierne? Did he mean Ireland?

"Ierne of the green fields. Ierne of the brown waters. Ierne the thrice named. That catcher of dreams on the edge of the western sea where memory and artefact and tradition reach out from the past to shine a light on the present."

I interrupted. I couldn't help it, it was just so incredible. "Are you trying to tell me that your people came here? To these Islands? To Ireland?"

He nodded, the hint of a smile gracing his face. "A land tilled and fair, but labouring under dark clouds. Labouring under the cruel yolk of the Fir Bolg. Sharing the land was not something that occurred to either them nor us, and so battle was joined. Even after everything that had happened. After all who had died the first thing that we did when we arrived in our new home was to anoint it with the blood of those who lived there. Some few amongst us objected."

His eyes met mine, anguish writ large. "This was not who we were!! But we had changed. Had been changed. Those long years of wandering had lessened us to the point where we were no better than those who were once our charges. It was at that point that something inside me broke. Which started me on the path I have trod ever since. I try and stay true to the beliefs as I was taught them. Back home. Back in the lands which are lost." His voice dropped away to silence as he remembered events which had taken place so long ago that to measure the passing of time in years would have no meaning.

"Those battles were fiercely fought, and no quarter was asked or given. The rivers ran red with blood until finally there dawned a day when at last the Fir Bolg stood at bay on the southernmost shore. Vanquished and diminished they took ship and fled into the western sea, following the trail of the setting sun. They fled into legend where, even yet, they abide.

He stood and turned away, staring into the sun. The moment dragged out to the point where I though he had finished. He couldn't stop there!! There were still things I wanted to know!! "What happened Bran?"

"My people celebrated." I was not prepared for the loathing which had infected his voice. "For the love of the goddess they celebrated! We, who had once counted all life as sacred, celebrated the slaughter of a people who had done naught but defend their homes. By the strength of our arms and the light which was within us we prevailed, though from that day forward that light was diminished and eventually died."

He sighed. "If only you could have seen it, Jen. Finias, a city built of glass, the sun reflecting off its golden spires, its walls faceted like a diamond then, when the sun set, it was lit from within by a thousand fires, every flame broken and magnified, scattering rainbows into the night. It was a sight to behold. A sight never to be seen again for they are lost to us. Lost to this mundane world of men. But all of this was long ago." He offered me his hand and helped me to my feet, "I was but a boy when we left. Apprenticed to the guild of craftsmen, I become a stone carver and so I have remained. The least, and the last, of those who came to Ierne."

I was having real trouble grasping everything that he had told me. I opened my mouth to talk… To ask… And nothing was coming out. You have to understand, I'd been brought up to be completely egalitarian when it came to religion. If you believed then you believed, it wasn't up to me to dispute those beliefs or put anyone down for believing. I… Well let's just say that as far as I was concerned, seeing was believing. Being open minded is all well and good but here…

Here was a man telling me that he was Tuatha. One of the Ancient Ones. Telling me, that to all intents and purposes, he was a god. Tell me, what exactly would you do?

"Are you trying to tell me that uh…. that you're a god??"

A frown appeared on his face. "Goddess forbid, have you learned nothing?? We were her chosen. She blessed us with gifts beyond that of humanity. We lived longer, were stronger, could do things…" He stopped and looked at me, "I can see why you might think such was the case and in truth, it was what led to our downfall.

"What do you mean" I was verbally nudging him, trying to get him talking again.

"Where we visited, we only ever intended to aid, to teach. To leave gifts and take only memories but these people looked on us and saw us as something we were not. There were those amongst us who were happy, nae, eager to play that role. To play god. And it is that which brought down upon us the wrath of the Goddess. I am just a man Jen. I will live for a long time by your reckoning. Perhaps I will live forever, but I am not Immortal. That curse is reserved. Even by the standards of my people I am no longer young. I can remember Leonidas standing with his 300, unbowed and defiant in the face the Xerxes immortals. I can do things which up until last night I would have said were beyond your ability," to emphasise his point, he snapped his fingers and a flame leapt from his hand to be just as quickly extinguished, "but let me be absolutely clear. I am NOT in any way, shape or form, a God."

It was too much. I'd been wrong, sooo so wrong. I shouldn't have asked. I could feel my brain starting to go numb to the relentless flow of information. I nodded, trying to process it all. "But what about… What was it…? Nuada?? Ogma?? Who are they, that you should be so scared of them?"

Ok... In hindsight "scared" might not have been the best choice of words given that we were being all touchy feely and open and sharing and stuff.

"Nuada," he growled.

I kid you not. he actually growled. It was... Interesting.

"Nuada Airgeadlamh. Royal Nuada. Noble Nuada. Him of the silver hand.' Was that a hint of bitterness I heard in his voice? Our people, yours, and mine, their first meeting in this land was not a happy one. You arrived on our southern shore and as so often happens, history repeated itself. We looked on your people and laughed. How could such a feeble folk hope to challenge our might. We who had defeated the Fir Bolg. And yet we had failed to recognise a simple truth. We were not what we once were. The forces of the king were defeated. Again. And again. Humanity had come of age. The students now stood eye to eye with the teachers. Amerghin and his brothers forced a truce upon us and gave us a choice. Surrender our treasures and remove ourselves forever from the world of man or face extinction. We could have been friends. We could have lived in Ierne in peace, to the benefit of all, but no. It was not to be. Nuada it was who leapt at the chance to separate our people from your own. Who argued in favour of the creation of their cities underground."

"The Sidhe!!" I exclaimed

Bran nodded. "He thought that there they would live, free from responsibility and consequences. Using their gifts for their own benefit, living in splendour whilst the world above succumbed to darkness. He thought that there, in the Underland, they could regain their strength. That they could return, in the fullness of time, and take back that which had been stolen, Their land, their treasures, and their pride." He spat on the ground. "They deserve their fate."

"What do you mean?" My voice sounded small in the face of such revelations.

"Amerghin was not deceived." Bran shook his head. "We had taught your people well. Too well. He joined his voice with one of our own and brought down a curse upon the portals. A curse which would, in the fullness of time, forever deny access to this world. I say again. They deserve their fate. They betrayed their charge, and they forgot their oath. Already the Goddess's curse finds them. Their lands and their wombs are become barren, and they resort to stealing children."

"Stealing children? You don't mean...? His look was enough to silence me.

"Where else do you think all those tales of changelings come from? Do not talk to me of Nuada," he spat the last words like a curse.

"So..." I took his hand in mine... To calm him down if nothing else, "How is it that you came to be here? If your people voted to leave, how is it that you stayed behind?"

We were approaching the stones and he let go of my hand. I could finally recognise what it was in his face that was so different. It was memory. Years uncounted drifted across his face as he stood and stared at the circle of stones. "Have you any idea how long it took your ancestors to build this?" He asked, gesturing at the complex. "It took them thousands upon thousands of hours to drag the stones from where they lay or from where they were quarried and more to set them in place... some even spent thousands of hours digging ditches or raising banks and for what? To pay tribute to someone who could have done it for them in a couple of hours."

My ears popped and there was a sound like the echo of the biggest ever bell. On the very edge of my nerves, I felt the energy enter the circle. Each stone gaining an aura of startling green like the light of St Elmo's fire dancing round the masts of ships in a storm. Slowly, gracefully, majestically each stone shuddered out of the ground, shaking the earth from their bases. Higher and higher they mounted the air then with a discordant note they dropped back into their sockets. One on the side closest to me falling over and lying flat. "I am the very least of my brethren and yet..." He gestured at the stones. I got his drift. If he could do that and he was essentially just a craftsman. What wonders...

or horrors

...were the glittering host of his people capable of. "What I'm trying to say is that I can't fix your problems for you. I can guide and I can advise. I can even assist you but ultimately you and Aed and Caoilin and all the people of the Glen must fix these problems for yourselves. Time must play out as is ordained and for better or for worse it looks like you have been chosen to facilitate this.

I sat down on the fallen stone, just trying to get it all straight in my head. "I know it's a lot to take in Jen, but does any of that change how you feel about me?? Does it change who I am?" I shook my head, mutely. "I am who I am regardless of who I was."

"I think we need something to eat, and something to warm our feet," I said, lifting my booted foot, soaked through, from the walk across the field.

"Some things never change," he grinned. He sat himself down opposite me and made a magicians pass with his hand and a flame burst from the bare earth where it continued to burn merrily on its own. "As for food, I'm afraid you will need to make do with whatever you can find over there." He gestured to the lean-too built against a tree. "I am to be found here quite often," he explained.

Never one to deny my curiosity I went for a rummage... Food wise I acquired a loaf of bread and, I couldn't help but laugh, some bacon. Seems Bran had a bit of a thing for bacon. There were clothes, another pair of shoes and there, hanging on a peg, was my keyring. I lifted it and carried it outside, "I thought you were going to destroy this??

"Truth be told I was about to do just that when I became aware of your confrontation with Callie. Fearing the worst, I arrived just in time to witness your actions." Looking at it thoughtfully he asked, "Do you actually know what this is? As a stone carver I can't help but admire the skill it took to create this, I'm almost tempted to keep it, simply as an example of beautiful craftmanship. But I can't. It's more than just a beautifully carved stone. Perhaps you will more fully understand If I explain to you the significance of the spiral"

My hand raised to my cheek. "My tattoo..."

He coughed, looking almost guilty "It's not strictly speaking a tattoo... At least, not with you, but you'll understand more in time"

I'm pretty sure there was no pun intended but you can never be too sure with Bran.

He'd set up a large iron skillet over the flame and tossed in some bacon. "Where to begin...."

Chapter 14

"When my people departed these lands, it left, how would you say? A power vacuum. Foremost amongst those who felt that loss most keenly were the Draoidh or, as they were to become known, the Druids."

"The Druids??" I exclaimed. He nodded, "I'm afraid I have to take part of the responsibility for what they became... Before I interfered, they were just priests. They prayed to Brid, predicted the seasons, and remembered the histories. They were nothing special. Not really. Not until the arrival of Amerghin. He who had but recently, with his brothers, defeated my people and doomed them to a half-life lived in the Underland." He smiled. "He was a lot like you. He did something which was way beyond what he should have been capable of. It was only later, after much investigation that I discovered that he'd had help. We had been betrayed. He had been taught by one of our own; Brid."

After the battle Amerghin left Ierne and, under the direction of Brid, came to these lands, to Ynys Mon in the west and there he found the Druids. Already devotees of Brid, they were focussed on learning and passing on their ancestral knowledge, they had a purely verbal tradition and filidh would spend years, learning at their masters' feet, before going on a pilgrimage to the oak groves of their ancestors. For centuries, they had prayed, and she had answered. For hundreds of years, she taught them the ways of medicine and foresight and into this fertile soil came Amerghin."

He paused, taking a drink before continuing. "Over time he moulded them. Directed them. They became more and more focussed on the arcane. Hunting out secrets best left hidden. Reviving practises best left lost. Every generation they moved further and further from Brids' teachings and closer and closer to his. They made the same mistake that my own people had made. The same mistake that led to our downfall. Learning for personal gain. Knowledge purely for the sake of knowing. Hiding and hoarding what they knew rather than freely giving that which was freely gotten. Then one day, they awoke, and Brid was gone. They built fires and sacrificed and called to the heavens, but their prayers went unanswered. The whole culture was on the verge of collapse when I, with the swagger of ignorance, stepped into the void which she had left. Needless to say, it all went terribly, terribly wrong." He sighed, bitterly, "To say I was inexperienced in dealing with your people is an understatement."

I looked at him in bewilderment "What happened Bran? What did you do?"

He looked away, avoiding my gaze. "Ultimately, the whole time travelling thing is my fault. Up until that point travelling in time was something that was purely in the preserve of the Tuatha. Its more complex than that but I'm trying to simplify for your benefit. It was an ability we had used to aid in our task of teaching, and if we were no longer to be your guides then I was determined to give you the ability to guide yourselves. After all, what better way is there to prepare for the future than knowledge of the past? You could teach yourselves. They forbade me. Told me it couldn't be done. I did it anyway. How could I not? You were so desperate to learn! At first those they could, in no way grasp what I was telling them, Again and again I showed them. Tried to teach them. Every attempt ended in failure."

He removed the skillet from the flames and served up lunch, handing me a wedge of bread which hadn't existed until a moment before. I shook my head at the casual way in which he performed the impossible. He gestured at the fire. "I was starting to wonder if wielding this kind of power were actually within the capabilities of your people, you are so limited when compared with us. Something I didn't fully understand until then. Finally, just as I was beginning to despair, one of my students grasped the concept, grasped what it was that I was trying to teach them and actually did it. He shifted in time. Not far, but he did it. In that moment of triumph, I forgot myself and laid my hand upon him." I started at him blankly. "Can you not understand?" he asked. "My awen was upon me and I laid my hands upon him. I, for lack of a better term, blessed him. At that time, I had no idea what it was that I had done or that it would have such a profound and far-reaching effect."

I was utterly entranced by his tale, I could only watch in morbid fascination as he unloaded hundreds, maybe thousands of years' worth of guilt. Grateful that he finally felt he had someone in whom he could confide.

"I can still see it Jen, we were standing on the crown of rock, and he had just shifted, only very briefly but he had done it. The sun was setting, and the western see was ablaze with colour. I was overjoyed. I reached out and grasped his face between my hands. There was this sudden awful feeling in my mind, in my chest, as if my very life were being pulled from me. As I watched, his hair turned the colour of the sunset, gold turning to red. Briefly his eyes glowed as the power of inspiration burned through his body, changing him in ways, I knew not how, and which would not manifest themselves for many years. Indeed, some changes would not manifest themselves in him at all, lying dormant and becoming apparent only in his children or his children's children. Where my right hand had touched him, burned into the skin, burned into his very soul was a glittering golden spiral.

My hand flew to my cheek… "It was you!!! You marked us both the same!!! You did this to me!!! You changed me, the same way you changed him!!!"

"Yes, and no" he replied.

God!!! why couldn't it just be a yes or no answer. It was never one or the other with Bran!!! You see what I mean by infuriating??

"What I did that night, to you... Damnit Jen... Haven't you figured it out yet? The spiral was already there. You've been using the circles for years, without even realising it. The hearing of voices? The losing time? What did you think was causing it? Every time you wandered up to the circles they were reacting to your presence. Frankly I'm amazed that it's taken you this long to fall through. The moment I saw you crossing that field, when I saw how you were dressed and then when I saw your hair, I had a fair idea what had happened and what I would find when I touched your cheek. True enough, the moment my hand made contact It lit up like a Christmas tree. It's a part of you. It's always been a part of you. It's a part of your genetic memory."

"But that's not how genetics works!!" I cried out, "You can't scratch me and six generations later a descendant has the same scratch! That's not how it works!!"

175

"OK, maybe genetics is the wrong word but it's the closest I can think of to describe what's happening here. You've got the red hair. Did your dad? Your granddad? Your mum?" I shook my head. "And yet it has to come from somewhere." He was standing now, striding about the clearing, talking with his hands. In the normal run of things it would mean that someone, somewhere in your family's past had red hair. It's what your geneticists call a recessive gene. Only this time, the red hair is a symptom of something else. Less genetics, more... Magic...

I've heard my hair described as many things. Magic was NOT one of them.

"One of your ancestors hundreds, maybe even thousands of years in the past can be affected by it, touched by it, and see no effects. At all. Or in any of their descendants and then for some unknown reason it appears. But why now? Why you? Now that the end is finally in sight."

I wasn't entirely sure whether he was talking about his story or something else, but I shoved that thought to the back of my head and let him continue.

"Needless to say, all the other apprentices attributed his success to the spiral, bestowing upon it an importance that it never really merited, They couldn't entertain the thought that someone else could do something which they had so regularly failed at. That they might not be as talented, so they looked for another reason. They looked for a key. I think I mentioned this to you before, yes?"

I nodded…

"And you remembered? Amazing…." He smiled, the old Bran briefly reappearing before returning to the topic at hand. "Ok… Let's see. Basic principles. In order to use the circles and the stones effectively you have to believe that you can do it. It's that simple. It's all very well and good knowing the mechanics of the how and the where but if you don't believe then you can have all the tattoos, all the knowledge, all the power in the world and it won't make a damn bit of difference. It just won't work. What all the apprentices believed, was that you needed a spiral tattoo in order to be able to do it. And, because so many of them believed it, and so fervently... Fiction became fact. For them at least. And so was born the key.

He paused and took another drink before continuing. "Your ability... That is, your INNATE ability to use the portals comes from... Well, I guess you could say that it ultimately descends from your ancestors. My first apprentice..."

He had the grace to wait for me to stop choking on my lunch before continuing. "Don't look so shocked. For some reason that I can't fathom, and I think we have established I'm not exactly the sharpest tool in the box, it's not something that shows up in every generation. It didn't with your dad, it didn't with your granddad but one look in the mirror, one look at that flaming red hair told me immediately that you were different. And not only that, it told me why. All I had to do was touch my finger to your cheek and, as I said before, it lit up like a Christmas tree."

He sat back down, prodding the cremated remains of the bacon... "And that is what I meant this morning when I said I was *almost* your uncle. I might not be related to you by blood, but I AM responsible for who you are, for who you turned out to be. And until you can use the gifts that have been given you, then you are my responsibility."

He shook his head and sighed. "All of that being said, you still shouldn't have been able to do what you did last night." There is something else going on here that I don't understand

and that makes me nervous." He lapsed into silence, staring at the fire.

This was absolutely huge... And I mean proper huge. I thought I'd feel better when I had all the facts, but I didn't, I just felt utterly bewildered. "You're still not telling me everything about yourself and your people though, are you?" I accused. His eyebrow lifted and a smile appeared,

Have I mentioned that feeling of the sun coming out? I have?

"That is as may be Jen, but that was the deal which you agreed to. Anything else you want to know will need to be learnt without guidance from me."

I only really have one more question, if you can answer it fine, if not..." I left it hanging. Taking his silence as consent I pushed on, "What made you stay behind when your people left?

He was silent, staring into the fire, lost in memory before answering. "My people had changed, and not for the better. Can you imagine that, Jen? People you had known your whole life just changing. Not suddenly, but by inches until one day you wake up and they are no longer those you had known. No longer those you had loved. They had stopped being the people I knew. The people I remembered. They had lost their way and were turning inwards. No longer was it their primary purpose to help develop the races of man but to enrich and advance themselves. They did this through force or intimidation or just outright theft. I left because I felt that I no longer belonged. That I no longer had a home amongst them." He shrugged. "I tried to council change, but my voice counted for little and so I did the only thing that made any sense to me. I left."

And with that, the moment was over. Anything else I wanted to know would have to wait. I now understood more about my family history than I ever expected to, but at least I KNEW and for that I was grateful. "Come on, we should get back before Balach comes looking for us, the day is passing, and I have no doubt that Aed will have managed to gather quite a crowd."

Bran stood and helped me to my feet, "You're right, but I can't come with you to Dunadd.

I stared at him in shock,

He shrugged in apology before continuing. "There are things I must do, people I need to meet with. I will await you here. Events must unfold as foreseen, and I can have no part in them. You have everything you need to succeed."

"But…."

"You do!" He said quickly, cutting off my protest. "You have friends you can depend on, you have confidence and you have right on your side. How can you possibly fail?" This last was said with his usual one sided smile and a twinkle in his eye, damn him.

"Fine!" I snapped, feeling slightly abandoned, "Will I find you here later??"

He gave me a sad smile, "I'll be here Jen, have a little faith. Things will turn out as they must. Some sacrifices must be made but they are also a part of the great plan."

Shaking my head at this ambiguity I gave him my back and started back towards the croft.

******

The closer I got to home the more apparent it was that the small gathering had turned into something a little bit more... Substantial. By the looks of it Aed had raised the whole glen. Goddess!! There had to be close to a hundred people gathered in the field in front of my sanctuary. I spotted him standing over by the croft, talking with Balach,

Now, that was a friendship I hadn't foreseen and yet Balach idolised Aed and was treated as a younger sibling in return. At this point, I'm not sure I could have separated them with a crowbar.

Looking at the two of them I felt a dark shadow tiptoe through my mind and knew that was significant in some way but the more I tried to understand the quicker the feeling slipped through my fingers. Shrugging it off I approached my home.

"Dear god Aed, I thought we were going to try and keep it to an unthreatening minimum! The purpose here is to get Maelgwyn to talk with Aoife... To negotiate... Not to get them to shut the gates and hide behind their walls!!!"

"My apologies Gwen but rumour flies faster and with more purpose than your crow..." I glanced about, searching, and sure enough there it was, perched in the oak tree on the other side of the garden, I'd have been almost disappointed if it hadn't been there, I had even started to expect it. He shrugged but continued on "They have been arriving and gathering here since not long after you left. They know that something is in the wind. Change IS coming and I think it's fair to say that they've all had enough."

Once again, I could feel the presence of them in my mind. It was like an extra sense. That feeling I'd had from the night before, the consciousness of the mob. I could actually feel it, leaning first one way, then the other. It was like the sea... First swelling and surging, then receding, and like the sea once it started moving in a particular direction then it would be unstoppable. It would sweep everything before it. I needed to cut this off right now. I would NOT let this get out of control in the same way that it had the night before. The emotion of the crowd was starting to slop over the edge of awareness, so much so that even Aed could feel it. Like that feeling you get before a storm. "You should talk to them Gwen, they'll listen to you." I pulled Curach over to the entrance to the field and climbed aboard.

He was a gorgeous wee horse but by the goddess he was round…

From this height I could look out over them… Farmers for the most part though here and there I could see swords. A small scattering of spears. Warriors come to play. This did not bode well. I could see more people approaching from the north. More from the south down by where Poltalloch would be. Great goddess what had we started.

I looked at Aed, he shook his head and motioned me to stand up… "Are you kidding me? You want me to stand? On a horses back?" I shook my head. Vehemently. "Are you crazy?"

He laughed, "Its fine, he's a calm sedate horse and he's been trained so just climb up, plus, the sight of you, dressed in white, standing on the back of a black horse will bring the crowd to silence. Trust me Gwen, I know my people."

And so, with the grace of one born to the saddle (ahem) up I stood, my arms frantically windmilling. Thankfully no-one seemed to notice. So here I was… Standing on the back of my horse. Being ignored. Or so I thought.

K. Baxter

It started like a ripple of sound at the back as someone noticed. Then another. And another. I could see it spreading. I could actually feel the emotions change... I let it wash over me, allowed it to buoy me up. I held up my arm...

I don't know why, it just seemed appropriate at the time.

...and on wings of midnight the crow glided down and settled on my wrist. You could hear a pin drop, I swear to god.

What in god's name was I going to say?? I searched my memory for something, anything that would fit the occasion.

"You have gathered here today to see that justice is done. To ensure that life and liberty returns to the glen, to the people." I could feel the effect that my words were having on the crowd. "Make no mistake, those who have afflicted the peace of this place shall be dealt with, but it will not be accomplished with violence, and it will not be accomplished with killing. We gather here in fellowship. In common purpose and unity, to do what must be done."

The wind blew across the field bringing hints of the forest and the sea beyond. I could feel the very nature of this most beautiful of places infusing me. Fortifying me for the days that were to come. "Only by standing together can we succeed this day. We go now to Dunadd to talk, and it is through talking that this thing will be done. It is by talking that we will succeed. Violence has no place in the soul of man. Violence begets violence and as strong as we feel standing here today, we are not strong enough to win this fight through violence, and so we go to talk. We go to persuade. We go to demand. The fact that we go armed is only to ensure that they listen. Not to provoke, because on such a day that we provoke a fight then we all lose. And I refuse to lose!! Not this time. Not to her. Who is with me????"

Circles and Stones

It was a paltry speech at best, cobbled together from books I'd read and movies I'd seen, barely worthy of the occasion but the roar which erupted nearly knocked me off my perch...

The crow took flight and circled the crowd in silent benediction then took wing, flying off to the south, towards Dunadd. The people streaming out behind it.

Chapter 15

It wasn't a great distance from the sanctuary to Dunadd and as such it wasn't long before a rider approached with a challenge as to our intentions. Aed spurred his mount to the fore. "We come to see the King and to speak with his counsellors"

I nudged Curach forward, Facing the messenger I said, "Please inform the priestess and Maelgwyn that we shall await their presence at the ford"

"And it please you Lady, Her holiness...

I almost choked at hearing Callie described as that

"...is currently indisposed. I am empowered to invite you and some small number of others to the Fort proper, there to discuss terms."

I glanced at Aed who gave a small nod. "We shall come, please inform your Lord that we shall join him on the morrow."

See!!! I could mangle language just as well as any of these guys.

I guess, now that it was official that we should come up with some sort of plan... I turned to Aed, "Could you go and find Aoife and Caoilin and bring them here? Actually, you'd better bring Balach as well, not that we'd be able to keep him away, I swear, he follows you about like a puppy."

Aed laughed, "he does at that, he's a good lad."

"I wouldn't let him hear you saying that he definitely considers himself more than a lad... He is not going to take kindly to being left behind"

Aed nodded, "I agree, with both sentiments. He will not take kindly to it, but it is the right thing to do. For all that we are just planning to talk, plans have a habit of falling apart with you." I woulda said something clever, but truth is truth. I was never one for plans, I was always more a seat of the pants kinda girl. You'll get used to it in time.

It wasn't long until we were joined by our fellow rebels. Aed took centre stage. "Ok... Now we know that Jens erstwhile friend is currently indisposed so there should be no problems in getting Aoife in to talk with Maelgwyn."

"But..." Aoife looked frankly terrified "But... what am I to say?"

I shrugged my shoulders... "I don't know, improvise. I think right now the main thing is just to get him talking. Once you've managed that then we can reason with him. This... " I gestured at the improvised warband, "has managed to get us an invite and, hopefully, safe passage" I looked Aed for confirmation, who nodded. "Not even she can change that. As a messenger and priestess both, whilst under the roof of the King, your life is inviolate. You will be able to have your say and be on your way. Until you leave the lands of the King, or the sun has set on the day of your departure your safety is guaranteed. On the Kings Honour."

I looked at our little group. "Ok. myself, Aed, Aoife and Caoilin will go up to the fort. You, Balach, are to stay back with your brothers to control the mob." He started to complain but subsided at a frown and a shake of the head from his mother.

I guess that settled the question on who wore the trousers in that household.

The sun was sinking low in the western sky, the islands of the Inner Hebrides silhouetted against the darkening sky. We stopped and made camp within sight of Dunadd. It sat there, rising like the boss of a shield above the surrounding land. It was possibly one of the more unassailable places I've ever seen. The fort itself wasn't hugely impressive but when you considered the surrounding land within which it sat... All I can say is that Aeds ancestors must have been inspired. Assaulting this place with force would do nothing except get a lot of people, mostly my people, killed. I sighed, shut my eyes, and turned my face to the fire.

Sleep came late. My over-active mind filled with distractions; Sights and sounds, shouts and whispers, voices shouting things I could not recall upon waking, but which left me feeling disturbed and apprehensive. The morning had dawned damp and misty... The land wrapped in a gown of white... As far as the eye could see, in any direction, the mist hugged the contours of the ground creating an unearthly, otherworldly feeling. Today was the day when we would hopefully get this whole mess sorted. I had absolutely no idea what we were gonna say to persuade granddad to take Callie and leave, I had no idea if he even would, but this was our chance. He couldn't have changed that much between now and when I would know him. Surely... I mean, he could argue with the best of them, but he was always willing to listen to reason. He was, well he would be, my granddad. I would find a way.

The crow dropped silently from the sky and alighted on my shoulder, I'd ceased even being surprised by its presence, but it was comforting, nonetheless. Ignoring the damp, I pulled on my boots and headed down to the river. It dawned on me that I had been here before. It had been here that Bran had stopped the river so I could see my new tattoo. It was a mark of how far I had come that the coincidence didn't even surprise me. As I got closer, I could hear voices echoing out of the fog.

"Hold it up just a bit higher... That's right... Lower your wrist... Lower... Now, follow my movements..."

I could see shadows ahead of me... Two bodies, arms outstretched, dancing in harmony. Arms weaving an almost hypnotic pattern, bodies moving slowly and gracefully in sync'. It reminded me of sitting watching Tai Chi in the park, back home. The mist thinned and I stepped forth to be confronted by Aed and Balach, swords in hand. They stopped as I approached. "Good morning your holiness," murmured Balach, lowering his eyes. "Good morning, Jen!" hailed Aed...

I'd very quickly discarded my alias and at my request everyone had started calling me by my actual name. All the holiness, Priestess, Jen, Gwen etc was more than a little bit confusing.

"I was just trying to teach out future captain of the guard how to use the sword which he insists upon wearing. I think we'd all much rather that he didn't accidentally kill one of us whilst he is waving it about."

"Fingers crossed we won't actually have to kill anyone" I muttered.

His face had taken on a sombre look. "In all seriousness Jen, despite what Bran said, I think you need to be prepared for at least the possibility of violence. I have the worst feeling that today won't pass without some form of bloodshed"

I threw up my hands "I know, I know, but hear me now Aed, the one thing you absolutely must accept, is that Callie is not to be harmed in any way."

"But wouldn't it just be better for all concerned if we just..." Balach's voice trailed off and he resumed staring at his feet. He had been quiet since we left the sanctuary. I guess the enormity of what we were trying to accomplish could silence even *his* normal chatter.

I placed my hand on his shoulder, "She will be dealt with at the proper time and in the proper place, don't worry. She will be made to pay for her crimes. Just, not here, and not now. I give you, my word. I just need her kept out of the way and occupied whilst I try and engineer a conversation between your mother, and Maelgwyn."

It still felt really weird calling him that. Don't @ me. It does. He was always just 'adad to me.

"Right. If you boys are finished here, then let's get everyone up and ready and we can get this over and done with."

We didn't even need to raise our voices, when we returned to camp, everyone was up. In the middle of the chaos, standing like a rock in the centre of a hurricane was the calm reassuring presence of Aoife. Directing, controlling, chiding. If things had been different, she would have made a fine general. I could feel her strength reaching out to me even here. Feel it wrapping me in warmth, it was something she'd always managed to do. Make me feel welcome. Make me feel loved. She saw me as I was, a sometimes scared, quite often confused 15-year-old, and yet gave me the respect of what I'd been forced to become, a priestess with the fate of the whole glen, grasped in my oft times shaking hands.

She was the strong base of everything I had done, was attempting to do. She gave me the confidence to believe that I could do it and that even if I failed then it didn't matter. She would still be there for me. I could understand how and why Balach was the boy he was and would be the man that he was becoming. Aoife was truly the heart and soul of my adopted family.

In what seemed like too short a time we were mounted and heading south. We would cross the river and swing out to the west and circle round and approach the crag from the East. Being in view the whole time that we were approaching put us at a tactical disadvantage, thankfully we were well out of range of anything they could throw at us until the very last minute.

Aed pulled his horse in beside mine and nodded out into the marsh, I looked, and there, seeming to stand on the very surface of the water was a lone figure. Too tall to be Callie, Too slight to be Maelgwyn. It was standing with both arms above its head, a staff held between. As the mist swirled and parted I could see more... One... Two... Three more standing. All with staffs raised. Aed whispered, so as not to be heard by those coming up behind. "It appears that the ancient ones have come to bless your undertaking and to pay homage. If even they are taking an interest in your comings and goings, then your fame has indeed spread far"

K. Baxter

"Who are they?? I whispered, my eyes never leaving the figures in the marsh."

"When we arrived from Ierne, driven forth by the never-ending battles waged on the southern plains, we found a people already here. They were a people slight of stature and with bodies painted in a myriad of designs. They lived in the forests and worshipped a god called Epwos. Indeed, that was what they called themselves. The Epwose. The people of the horse. As we pushed further and further inland, they retreated deeper into the forests, the mountains, and the marshes. Occasionally someone encounters them, but they vanish as quickly and as silently as they appear. Indeed, they are quickly becoming more myth than man and the people hereabouts hold them with suspicion. They are often viewed as a herald of doom. Or fortune. Or both." He shrugged at my questioning look. "People can be fickle. To see four at once, and four of their priests no less, is a rare occurrence. Tales will be told of this day Jen. Filidh will sing of your deeds through the length and breadth of these islands." I punched him in the arm. He laughed.

Finally, we were approaching the gates at the base of the fort and once again I was struck by how imposing it would look to anyone coming here with anything other than good intentions. Aed motioned us to dismount. "From here I'm afraid we will need to proceed on foot."

As we neared, the great gates of oak swung open on silent hinges, and there in the opening stood the King and, standing within touching distance was Maelgwyn. Aed strode forward and wrapped his father in a hug. "Good day to you father, we have come that we might have words with your counsellor" He nodded towards Maelgwyn.

This was the point that we'd been discussing and planning for. Hoping against hope for that perfect moment. Maelgwyn stared down at us. "There is nothing that we need to talk about..."

The moment he stopped speaking I nudged Aoife out in front. She was dressed in her everyday clothes and her hair was gathered, simply, at the back of her neck. She looked as she did every day, but Maelgwyn stopped as though struck dumb. "Aoife!" he gasped, his face reddening. "What... What are you doing here? If SHE sees you!"

She walked forward her hand reaching out "Gwyn... We need to talk to you, I need to talk to you, Please... Please don't turn me... Turn us... Away."

He looked stricken. Torn. Abruptly, he nodded, spun on his heel, and led us into the fort.

******

We were gathered in the great hall. Suddenly we had our moment, and I had no idea what I wanted to say. Aoife and Maelgwyn were sitting, hand in hand just staring at each other. I mean, I've heard of being star struck but this was taking it to a whole other level.

Enough was enough, we had a limited window of opportunity here. "I hate to... Uh... Disturb you, but we really need to talk. What I'd really like to happen here is for you to take your friend and leave this place. Take her and go. The last thing I want is for this to descend into a fight so if we can settle this without bloodshed then that would be to everyone's benefit."

He tore his eyes away from Aoife's face and looked at me, "Why exactly are you talking to me about this? If we are to leave this place, then it is not I before whom you should be laying your plea. It is her..."

I frowned, "But I thought... I mean we assumed, that after the other night... She would be indisposed, as it were. She appeared to be quite... Distraught, when last we met."

He laughed, bitterly... "She is always distraught of late. These past few months it is as though something inside her has broken. She was always of a cruel and calculating disposition but had, until recently, managed to hide it behind a facade of civility. I wish you to know, her actions that night were as much a shock to me as they were to you."

"Then why do you follow her, beloved?" Aoife had entered the fray. "Surely you can see why her rule must end. If not here and now, with talk and reason, then tomorrow, or the day after, but with sword and fire? Why do you follow her when you know what she does is wrong?"

Right at that moment I think Aoife could have persuaded trees to pull up their roots and go plant themselves in another field. She was heart stopping. What she felt for this man was written in every move that she made. Her heart beating with every word, her emotion reaching out to touch everyone in the room.

He had extracted his hands from Aoifes grasp, and they lay clenched on the table. "I cannot help it. Many years ago, when we were young," he laughed bitterly, "Young... We were hardly more than children. We lived in the same village. We were friends..." He paused, "that's not quite how it was... She was my friend... I was... Simply a means to an end, something that became ever more apparent as the years rolled by. Even back then she was stronger willed than I. The days passed, the sun shone, and the rain fell. It was an ordinary life and in our own way we were happy. Until that day when they came.

When the Romans came." There were gasps of disbelief around the table. He smiled wryly "Did I not tell you I was from far away my love?"

He stood and gathered himself, his arms crossed, his head bowed. When finally, he lifted his gaze it was to stare right at me. "My name is Maelgwyn ap Gwion and I was born in a village on the Island of Mona in the seventh year of the reign of the Emperor Claudius. When I had 12 summers, the Romans attacked. My parents were killed, my brother, my sisters. All dead. The nemeta, the sacred groves of oak were reduced to ashes, the druids were slaughtered, the cromlechs destroyed. I was trapped in my home, the flames spreading into the thatch... The smoke searing my lungs. I prepared myself to die, calling on our ancestors to guide my way when, in the darkness, a hand took hold of mine..." She had rushed into the burning house and pulled me out. I would have died there had it not been for her. We two alone survived the burning and eventually we fled our Island home and spent the next, I don't even know, months? Years? Running, hiding... Briefly we found a haven, somewhere to rest and recover but not even that could last and eventually we had to leave. We fled north. Ever north. You see, we were searching. Searching for something, a weapon... Knowledge... Something that could help us...

He sat back down and resumed his grip on Aoifes hand. We were looking for something we could use to save us and our people. But she is no longer the girl I knew growing up. She has become something else. Something cold and hard. He shuddered. "From the moment she saved me from that burning house, we were tied together. I owe her a debt of life. A debt that I can never repay unless in kind. As the years passed our paths diverged but from that moment onwards, I was hers to command. He dropped his gaze from me and looked at Aoife. "There is nothing... Nothing that I can do.

Honour requires that I obey her even when my soul is dying within me."

"Oh, my love" whispered Aoife, her voice filled with emotion. She wrapped her arms around him and held him tight. An action he hesitantly returned.

Disentangling himself from Aoife he again looked at me. "But you... You know her from somewhere else, do you not? Every time you speak of her it is written all over your face. In your eyes. And yet that cannot be true. In all the years that we have travelled together I do not recall having ever encountered you, and yet you do know her. Don't you?"

I smiled at him. "Would it shock you to know that I also come from a great deal further away than the top of the glen?? Where I am from, she calls herself Callie and for the last couple of years I considered her to be my friend, and even more recently, my teacher. Then for some reason involving you she changed. She kept saying I would figure it out and became totally irrational. That was when she attacked me, and I ended up here, with no way of knowing where I was or how I was ever going to get home."

"Wait..." he had immediately picked up on my error...

Way to go Jen!!!

"...Involving me?? His face was puzzled. "How could it involve me? You and I have never met."

I decided to just go for it. "Yet... We haven't met yet. We will... Or have... No. We will. Damnit. This still hurts my brain. Suffice to say that we will know each other but that is truly all I can say. Creating a paradox is the last thing I need to do. Bran would kill me"

Circles and Stones

"You know of the Lord Bran?? he looked startled, "It is
long since I have heard his name. My village and all those
nearby paid homage to him with tribute and sacrifice. His
worship has long since faded in these lands, but it is through
his teachings that we can travel the paths of air and
darkness."

I think I JUST about managed to stop my mouth from
dropping open. Aed was not so lucky. "Wait... Are we talking
about the same Bran?" I'm staring at him frantically willing him
to shut up, to change the subject, anything...

"You have heard of his teachings then?" Maelgwyn smiled
in what seemed to be genuine pleasure. "It is rare indeed to
encounter any who remember him. It is said that the ancients
still revere him, but they are rarely to be found in these lands
in this day and age."

Thankfully Aed had noticed my not-so-subtle messages
and had shut his mouth. I had no idea why but suddenly I
knew it was of vital importance that they not know about Bran.
As far as anyone was concerned Bran was just another man.
A hermit. Maelgwyn was looking around the table, he sighed.
"I know it is not what you wish to hear, and it is far from my
heart's desire, but I cannot in good faith go against her
wishes..." He trailed off... His gaze going to the window.

From outside I could suddenly hear what our conversation
had hidden. Shouting. The sound of metal on metal and the
mob. I could suddenly feel it in my mind, a sluggish heaviness
weighing on my thoughts, a collective consciousness
suddenly aware of its own strength... Flexing its muscles as it
smashed through the line of guards at the gate and surged
into the lower levels of the castle. I could feel it seeking...
Searching... I could feel the sparkling burst of triumphant
energy as it found... Something... Someone...

The door slammed open, and a guard rushed in. "Treachery my lord! They have taken the gates!" He stopped, struggling to catch his breath. "They have taken the gates and occupied the lower levels... And my Lord," His face, white with fear... "They have taken the priestess."

Chapter 16

Maelgwyn was on his feet, glaring at me, "Betrayal!!! Was this your plan all along?? To distract me with love and sympathy all the while planning to accomplish with violence that which you could not achieve with kind words and flattery??

"It was never our intent my love" retorted Aoife, but if you had a mind of your own then you would know that this was always a possibility. Did you really think I would come here without planning for this eventuality? Without knowing that, if we were ever to be together, then the hag must die? Did you consider me too weak to fight for what I want? I am a warrior's daughter and a warrior's mother and I know well how to fight for those that I love, and I love you, Gwyn. It is a flame which has burned in me since the day I first saw you. I may have been able to smother it, hide it, even forget it, for a while, but I could never quench it. Come with me my love. Come with me and we can leave this place. Leave her. We can be together. We can be a family."

She had crossed the floor and had his hand gripped between hers. They stood there, locked in an eternal moment, staring into each other's eyes. In that moment, nobody else existed. It was just Aoife. And Maelgwyn. The passion in her voice filled the entire room "Please Maelgwyn, please come home."

You could have heard a pin drop. And then it was over. He leaned forward, kissed her gently on the forehead and strode from the room.

What had just happened, I looked around, completely lost for words. We'd planned for this. We wanted... Needed, Aoife to talk to Maelgwyn, but I don't think any of us expected this!

The noise from outside slowly began to drown out the sound of Aoife's tears... Damn him! He can't just leave... How could he just walk out and leave her?

No! This is not how this ends!!!

I jumped up and headed for the door, running before I was even out of the room. The sight which greeted me was one of chaos.

The lower levels were seething with people... A maelstrom of anger and hatred and there, in the eye of the storm, was Callie. Blood running down the side of her face. The mob had her tied to a pole in the middle of the courtyard, logs, brushwood, peat, anything that would burn, already stacked around the base. It didn't take an idiot to figure out what was about to happen. And it WAS going to happen. I could feel it. I could almost see the future starting to take shape. I could feel the paradox hanging over me like some kind of temporal Sword of Damocles. I had no idea what would happen to my future if Callie somehow died here, but I was betting it wasn't good.

Circles and Stones

The atmosphere was at fever pitch. I could see Balach standing there, torch in hand, his brothers marshalling the rest of the people. I can't believe I didn't see this coming from the very beginning. That Aoife might have a completely different goal than the rest of us and had engineered this whole thing from the very beginning. Balach on one side. Maelgwyn on the other. One fighting his way through the crowd, trying to reach the pyre, the other, flaming torch, gripped in his hand, being pushed forward. It was a sign of how conflicted I was that I didn't know who I wanted to reach Callie first.

It had to be Maelgwyn. It HAD to be. As much as I knew Callie to be a hopeless cause she could not be allowed to die here. Bran had said that she would meet her doom, in the proper time and at the proper place, and I was pretty sure that neither of those were here and now. I stood on the wall, my arms and eyes raised to the heavens, praying to all the gods, to ANY god for a miracle...

The rain started as a light drizzle.

Rain?? Really?? This is Scotland!! I'm not sure that really counts as a miracle!

It was too late. As those first drops started to fall Balach reached the pyre and thrust the burning brand deep into the kindling and the whole thing just burst into flame.

I could feel the energy of the crowd surge. It washed over me like the tide, weakening my already tenuous control. My mind echoed it with a surge of its own. I was rocked back... It was happening again... Like the other night. I could feel it. I couldn't afford to lose control like that again. Too much depended on what we were trying to do. Blood was dripping from my hands from where my nails had dug into the palms and with every drip, I felt the power flare and diminish.

I could breathe again… My vision was returning to normal. Things were no longer outlined in sparkles. If I could just get their attention, I might… MIGHT be able to reign in the crowd but it was like trying to hold sand in my hand. Bits and pieces kept slipping through my fingers… But I had reckoned without Maelgwyn. He had fought his way to the pyre and was pulling burning logs out with his bare hands. Tearing apart the fire that threatened to immolate Callie. By now she had stopped screaming and was just kinda hanging by her wrists. With a final effort Maelgwyn scattered the last of the burning fuel and cut her down. The look on his face was terrible to see. The courage it must have taken, given his history, to wade into the fire to save her…

Wait… It suddenly dawned on me the import of what had just happened… He had saved her. HE had saved HER! He had SAVED her.

Oh my god!!

A debt that could never be repaid except in kind…

He was free!!!!

I don't know if he knew or if he understood what had just happened but oh my giddy aunt, he was free!

He was free to do what he wanted, be with WHO he wanted. He could leave her. One look and it was clear that Aoife understood what had happened. Hope battled with fear in her eyes as we all stood and watched him approach… Watched him climb the stairs with Callie cradled in his arms.

******

She was unconscious. As soon as he walked in, he laid her, not ungently, on the floor. Kneeling, head bowed, he checked for a pulse.

Satisfied, he stood, seeming to grow taller by inches, his shoulders straighter than I'd ever seen. He turned to face us, tears streaming down his face. He held his hands out to Aoife. "I think I'd like to go home now. If you'll still have me?"

"If she'll still have you?" Callies voice cut through the joy of the moment like a sharp knife through butter. "If she'll still have you?? Your heart and soul belong to me Maelgwyn. We are tied together for all time by a debt you can never repay! Through fire you have passed and survived. All by my hand. Your survival this long is down to me. ME!! Who was it that saved you when you had given up? Who was it who dragged you from the Fire? Your life belongs to me, and you will do my bidding!!" She motioned at Aoife. "Kill her. Kill them all. Let us be done with this wretched place."

He looked at her... I could see the compulsion wash over him, his eyes flickering for a moment then... Nothing. He straightened, facing her. "No."

Her eyes blazed "KILL THEM!!! You cannot resist, I saved you! You are bound to me! Bound to my will!!! Bound by a debt that you can never repay!!"

"Bound by a debt which I have repaid!! Pulling you from the flames was my last act of servitude to you. Pulling you from the fire when every part of my body cried out to let you burn has settled the debt between us. Never again shall I do your bidding Beira"

So yeah, turns out Beira was her real name.

K. Baxter

"We are the last of our people and through your actions, you now stand alone. I am the last of those who could have absolved you of your crimes, but I cast you out. I deny you the solace of your ancestors. I deny you the shelter of my heart. I cast you out and condemn you to exile for so long as you draw breath."

He stood before her now, his words striking truer than any sword. "No people. No home. I cast you out! Leave this place Beira. Leave this place and these people. Leave, and be damned."

Turns out 'adad had a poetic turn of phrase when he put his mind to it. Who knew?

He turned to Aoife, "I ask you again, Will you have me?? I am not the man that you knew, I am not even the man that I was, but I think together we could discover who I am and if you'll have me, we can discover, together, what we could become.

Aoife burst into laughter as she pulled him to her. "You will always have a place with me my love. Always and forever."

The realization hit Callie like a blow, it took her a moment I think before she fully understood what 'adad had said... She literally went from sitting on the floor being generally unpleasant to a howling spitting she demon in like ten seconds flat. She launched herself directly at Maelgwyn, knife in hand...

Oh my god... Where did she get a knife!! Why didn't we check her for weapons when she came in??? 'adad was standing there, back turned, unarmed and unarmoured. Everything just seemed to slow down. My future was hanging by a thread, and I stood frozen. Paralysed by what I could see was going to happen. The stone knife glittered in her hand

and in that instant, I knew exactly where I had seen it before. I'd held it gripped in my hand, blood running down my arm not more than a couple of months and 2000 years ago. I tried to cry out. I tried to warn him of what was happening, what was going to happen, but he just stood there. Oblivious. Attention completely consumed with a future that only he could see. A future which could never come to pass.

Finally, my body reacted. I was moving towards her but there was no way I could ever reach her in time. I could see the knife begin its downward arc and, in that moment, Aoife, wrapped in her beloved's arms for perhaps the first and last time, saw the danger. Holding him to her, her arms wrapped tight around the man she loved, holding tight to the man for whom she had raised an army and stormed a keep, a man for whom she had been prepared to kill. Holding him tight to her breast she fixed her eyes upon his, fixing his face in her mind, and spun.

I was too late.

The knife took her right between the shoulder blades.

Red bloomed. On her back and in my mind. A crimson flower of hatred blossomed at the core of my being. Burning brighter and hotter than the sun. I could hear myself screaming from a distance as my emotions threatening to spill over and destroy what little control I had. My screams hit her like a blow, smashing through her facade of supreme confidence. For the first time I glimpsed beneath the veil as fear filled her eyes. Real, honest, fear. For the first time I think she actually saw me, the veil, torn from her eyes.

I think even she could feel the power in my mind, straining against the bonds which I had set. I needed to release it. Holding onto it was eating away at my self-control... Burning channels in my mind... Changing me. I needed an outlet, or it would tear me apart.

I gave it to my hate.

Light and heat exploded from my mind. When I glanced down my hand was engulfed by a blazing globe of crimson light. I raised it higher. Fully intent on striking that face. Intent on wiping her from history.

I could do it. I knew I could do it. The information was there in my mind the moment I thought it. I no longer care about the paradox. I no longer cared what it would do. It had gone on far too long. To many people had suffered. Too many people had died. It needed to end....

"Jen......"

"She needs to die. She has to pay!!!"

"Jen....!"

"No!!!!!! please let me do this..."

"Jen...!" Bran's voice whispered in my mind. "Events must happen as they happened. Let her go. Time will not forget what she has done, and her fate is beyond what you could imagine... I would not have her final act of evil be that you lose yourself to the darkness."

"I need to do this" I sobbed.

I looked at her. The terror on her face plain for all to see. She had looked in my face and had seen her death. There was no denying it was an outcome I greatly desired, but I trusted Bran. If anyone would ensure that Callie paid for what she had done, then I trusted Bran. That being said, I was not above a little bit of vengeance. I think I was justified in that at the very least. I may have been forbidden to kill her but that left me quite a lot of wiggle room.

I gripped her wrist tighter, grasping her arm right over where the tattoo stained her skin and I willed it hotter... The fire in my hand burst forth anew, searing into her skin, distorting the pattern... burning the flesh. She was crying. Sobbing. Writhing in the pain as my thumb burned deeper and deeper into the arm. Deep inside, in the darkest corner of my mind something stirred and smiled at her pain. I let go, recoiling from the horror of what I had just done, I felt my conscious thought rejecting, denying my actions but the darkness in my mind remained, as I knew it would for as long as I lived...

I pushed her away from me and snarled at her. "Go!!! Should I find you within the bounds of this valley come sun-up tomorrow then your life is forfeit. Go!! whilst I'm still minded to mercy." She staggered backwards, cradling her arm. "GO!!!! I screamed" and with that she fled.

I turned to find the hall staring at me. Fear on every face. Slapping my hand on my leg to extinguish the flames I staggered to 'adads side and sank to the floor.

He sat there. Aoife cradled in his lap. I could hear her breath rattling in her chest as she struggled to breathe, gasping with the effort, she lifted her hand to beckon Aed and Caoilin... "Please care for Balach. He is not yet old enough to understand. He will need you in the days to come, I think." To me she turned her gaze... Her eyes filled with love. "You are the daughter that I never had. This last month has been a blessing. I thank you for giving Balach a name and for giving me back my heart." Her eyes closed and her breathing grew ever more shallow... Finally, she opened them and gazed upon the face of the man for whom she had sacrificed everything… Whispering… "Always and forever my love."

She sighed as the wound stole away her life, all the pain, all her cares and worries melting away from her face. A lifetime of living replaced by a look of peace.

Chapter 17

The rain continued on and off for the rest of the day. Too heavy for mist but not quite rain it shrouded the valley in sadness. We searched for Callie, of course we did. How could we not. We searched all through the citadel and out into the surrounding lands but no sign of her was ever found, it was as if the land (or time) had simply swallowed her. Some time later, her horse was found wandering the moors up by the Cairnbaan stones which pretty much confirmed to me that she really was gone.

Conlann was as good as his word and stepped down in favour of Aed and the people of the Glen celebrated as the word spread of the success of the rebellion (as it became known). A success it was, but the cost had been high, some would say too high and right at that moment in time, celebrating was the last thing on our minds. After some discussion It had been decided that we would take Aoife back to the cottage.

Her cottage.

Back to where she had made a home for herself, for her son, for me, and for anyone who happened to drop by. We would take her home and commit her to the care of her ancestors.

Hell, there was a big empty cairn at the bottom of the garden and if anyone deserved to be buried like a queen it was Aoife.

Maelgwyn... At dusk he had come to me. He stared at me, In fact he stared at me for so long that it began to feel more than a little bit awkward. Eventually, he spoke. "I am known to you." He held up his hand, silencing my imminent interruption. "I know not how or why, but we have a history together. I am something to you, above and beyond all this." he gestured at the surroundings and to himself. "Can you at least tell me when or even how?"

I shook my head... "I'm sorry but I can't." I wrapped my arms around him and held him tight, forestalling any argument he may have had. "All I can say is that we are... Or we will be, friends. I can't tell you more, I wish I could, but I came so close to messing things up, messing everything up. I just don't know what I can and can't tell you. There's so much that you just don't know yet "

"Yet???" he looked startled "You mean to say that you are from the days yet to come???" A wild hope had appeared in his eyes. "Can you at least tell me where SHE can be found, I would find her if I can, finish what you wouldn't..." The bitterness in his voice a lash to my already wounded conscience.

"It's not that I couldn't... You of all people must understand. The fact that I know her, have met her, in the future means that I couldn't kill her. I had to let her go. I Had to. You have my word that She WILL pay for what she has done. Even if it means I have to hunt her down myself. But in the here and now, I could permit no harm to come to her. Our paths will most likely cross again, of that I am sure, and if the time is right then nothing will stop me from making her pay for her sins."

"But what am I to do?? If I can't avenge her... If I can't honour her... What am I to do??" The pain he must have felt, breaking his voice. "Beira... Callie... She won't stay away. You may have beaten her, she may even be so scared of you that she leaves well enough alone, but I can guarantee you, that does not hold true for me. Once she has recovered her composure, she will come looking for me. Should I stay here, I will be a danger to all those whom you hold dear. As has already been shown." At this he just stopped, his voice choked off and he just stood and stared out over the marshes... Lost in memories of what should have been.

"You're right" I sighed. "Of course, you're right. It would be too much to hope, that she won't come back for us. You should leave. Go somewhere she would never think to look for you... Somewhere far far away. Go to the past... Or the future. Go to the circles and lose yourself in time, immerse yourself in a culture that's far from here. Somewhere that she will never find you. Take your memories of us and your love for Aoife and go." I pulled him close to me. "Aoife will always be here. You will always know where she lies. She will be safe, I make this vow to you. She will rest in peace."

He hugged me then and my heart almost broke. I'd had the nearest thing to my granddad returned to me and I was almost immediately sending him away. Sending him away as much for his own safety as for ours. He had to be given time to heal, to recover, and staying in the glen would accomplish nothing other than him becoming a lodestone to draw Callie back to where this whole thing could start again. I had not expended this much energy and lost so much that I wanted to go through it all again.

The following day dawned bright and clear, and it was a sadly diminished group that proceeded down from the citadel and out into the glen proper. Aoife was laid out in the back of the wagon. Balach, bowed and mute since I had broken the devastating news, sat up front with Caoilin and guided the horses. I rode honour guard with Aed, side by side, at the rear.

"What do you plan to do now?" he asked quietly... "Now that Callie is gone, I mean."

I stared at the ground rolling past beneath Curach's hooves. What WAS I going to do now? I really had no idea, no plan beyond yesterday. I shrugged, "I don't really know... I hadn't really thought beyond what happened yesterday, I really need to speak to Bran to see what happens now. To see if I have a home to return *to*."

"You could stay," he suggested gently. "Help us... Help me rebuild. The people trust you... You could do so much good, help so many people."

I laughed. "The people are afraid of me Aed, after what happened in the great hall, word will spread. I'll be lucky if they don't try and burn me as a witch. They don't respect me. They're afraid of me. There is a massive difference, and you really don't want that to be your legacy. About the best thing I could probably do for you right now is to leave. Let your father look after the farm, let him retire to his life of quiet contemplation. My sanctuary is a perfect place for him. Let him become, to the people of the glen, what I could never be. Could never become."

We'd reached the ford and had stopped. Barring our passage across the river stood two men and a woman. Aed rode forward and, fearing trouble, I nudged Curach into a walk and rode forward to join him. The last thing we needed, and frankly, the last thing I was in the mood for right now, was trouble. One of the men waded out into the river and crossed over, He bowed his head respectfully to Aed and turned to Balach. "We have come to bring her… To bring you… Home.

And so it went. Word had spread between the steadings of what had happened. What one of their own had done. What one of their own had sacrificed for them. Every couple of miles we were joined by more and more people. They came in pairs or in groups of three or more. From both sides of the glen, they gathered. From hill and moor they gathered. From coast and heath, they gathered.

They gathered and followed to pay tribute to one of their own. Following in silence until at last we stood at the gates to the farm. The women went first, preparing the way whilst the men lifted the flatbed off the cart and ever so gently carried Aoife to her final resting place.

In my day, Ri Cruin was a ruin. Dismantled, excavated, used for gravel extraction and as a kiln, but here today it stood unfinished. Two cists constructed in the middle surrounded by a ring of stones some 20 meters across. Standing at the cairn, waiting, was Bran. He stepped forward and lifted the body from the litter and carried her to the where she would lie. I stood, Balach's hand clenched in mine, tears streaming down both of our faces. Gently Bran placed her in the grave. In the tradition of the ancients, he raised his arms and his gaze to the sky and started chanting, in what language I knew not… The rhythm of the words tugged at my consciousness, voice after voice took up the refrain until the night sky was filled with song. Wave upon wave, rising up and echoing back from the surrounding hills, creating a wall of sound… I could feel it deep in my soul as It swelled into the night and slowly, but surely, the cap stone lifted from the ground, buoyed up by the combined emotions of those gathered round the cairn and lowered itself gracefully onto the grave. Flames leapt from the hilltop directly behind the farm, to be answered by another from across the way... And another, and another... Flames leaping from hilltop to hilltop carrying the news... One of their own had died for them, and tonight they gave her honour. Tonight, the whole glen mourned.

One by one or in twos and threes the crowd moved forward, every person carrying a rock, a stone, some bigger, some smaller. Each one placing it on the grave. One by one they came forward, paused, and placed their stone and their prayer beside or atop before moving on. Every one stopping to speak to Balach on their way past. By the time we were down to the last few the cairn was standing 9 feet high, a change also reflected in Balach, he was standing a little bit taller, his shoulders, a little bit straighter. The honour given his mother, lifting him up, helping him to understand what it was she had done, and why. Eventually the crowd dispersed, leaving a lone figure standing by the grave. Giving Balach's hand a final squeeze I walked down to the cairn. The smell of flowers and burning peat, strong in the evening air. Bringing back memories...

Aoife's frustration every time I burnt the dinner.

Aoife bedding in the fire before going to bed.

Aoife directing and controlling the mob.

Aoife, with the light leaving her eyes.

I stopped beside the figure. I knew he would come. There was nothing on this earth that could have stopped him. I slip my hand into his and looked up at his now familiar face. The face that had been there every day as I grew up. A face now stained with tears.

"I'm so sorry 'adad…"

<u>Chapter 18</u>

Together we left the cairn and, following Bran, we made our way slowly across the fields, following trackways made by the tread of bare feet then sandals then boots over thousands of years. Slowly but surely, we made our way to the Temple Wood. And as we walked, 'adad talked.

For those of you who are wondering. 'adad basically means Granddad. When I was tiny wee, I couldn't say it properly and it came out as 'adad. What can I say, It stuck.

"I awoke one morning, and I was aware that things were different. I could remember things that from my perspective had never happened. That's when I knew. Or, thought I knew. I thought that Beira had finally found a way to change time. Always before, no matter what we tried, where we tried it... It just created a ripple in time but nothing more. Everything just kept moving on as before. Yes, there were some minor changes but even those faded as time moved on. I came to believe that it was impossible. That everything we were doing, all the lives we were manipulating, all the people who had died... It was futile. All I wanted to do was to find a quiet decade somewhere, settle down and just fade into time but I couldn't. I was still tied to her by that damned blood debt. Eventually we came here and, well, events unfolded pretty much as you know except in the past which I remember... The baby died and the people rose in rebellion. Everything else is much the same but I couldn't understand why I could now remember two separate and distinct pasts. I could only conclude that she had found a way to change time. Never in my wildest dreams did I think that it was you. I had no idea that the priestess was you all along!! Why didn't you tell me???"

Bran snorted, "She couldn't tell you, you of all people should understand that. Time must move as it always has, as it always will."

"What did you do, yesterday. After you left?" I asked

"When I first left, I had every intention of finding Beira, and killing her. I had the knife she had used to kill Aoife and my mind was made up. I went straight up to Achnabreac, to the circles and just picked sometime at random and went... Time after time I heard rumour of her and again and again, I failed in my quest. After a while I started to feel guilty about all the lives we had ruined and I was determined to try and fix it, or at the very least help. I spent a lifetime and more just jumping back and forth in time. Helping where I could but eventually, she recovered, and the hunter became the hunted. Everywhere I went, she followed. Eventually I faked my own death and escaped into the future where... Well, I guess you know the rest. I met a beautiful lass with eyes the colour of honey. I had no desire or intention for what happened with Brienne but eventually this followed that, and we were married. Which, ultimately, led to you."

"Now... Forgive an old man his curiosity but how is it that you come to be here? From my perspective, I only left the village this morning. Your grandmother had but recently died, despite my best efforts to persuade her otherwise, and with her gone..." he sighed, "there was nothing keeping me from resuming my quest to try and stop Beira. Your father was married. He was happy, and you... He smiled, "You were everything I could ever have hoped you would be. You would be fine. It was finally time for me to leave, time for me to die. Her trail was long cold, so I came back to the very place where I knew she had but recently left. Somewhere I could easily pick up her trail and resume the hunt. Time had changed and she was the only one, as far as I knew, who could potentially do such a thing. I never for one second imagined that I would ever see you again. Especially here!"

"Well... Uh," I cast my mind back, a lifetime ago, when I found myself falling asleep on a hilltop, on a summers day 2000 years (or there abouts) in the future. "From my point of view, it's been three years since you left. Everyone said that you had died, but no matter how hard I tried to accept it, it just didn't ring true. It all started with me being expelled from school and being sent home early for the summer holidays." I ignored the frown which appeared on his face at the mention of my expulsion and ploughed on. "Mum and dad were their usual pre-occupied selves so I just spent most of my time down at the museum. Not long after you'd left a new curator arrived in the glen and had taken over at the museum. Her name was Callie. She was young and she let me into the museum when it was closed. We became really good friends. Or so I thought."

"Wait a minute... Callie???" He asked, frowning "Do you mean Beira??? She finally tracked me down??"

"Uh... Yeah, If I'm right she must have missed you by like a couple of weeks. It turns out that she goes by quite a few names. You knew her as Beira and the woman who I became friends with called herself Callie. But yeah. Both the same person. Anyway, it all came to a head when I found the stone

216

knife wedged into one of the standing stones here at Temple Wood and she started going all weird."

Bran scowled... "There is no stone knife wedged in any of the stones here at Temple wood. I'm pretty sure I'd remember such a thing."

"Anyway," I frowned at him for the interruption, "I pulled it out and cut my hand all to hell which, now that I think about it, is when Callie changed. She was terrified that I'd spill blood in the circle or something..."

Bran glanced at me; one eyebrow raised. When I indicated that I'd finished he continued. "Well," when it comes to the stones, those are slightly different to the circles in that... I'm sure I already told you this?"

I shook my head.

"Oh. OK then. The operation of the circles depends on belief. The stones are slightly different. They need blood. In order for you to be able to use the stones to travel you need to make an offering. A sacrifice. Goodness knows where Callie dug up that piece of information, it's not exactly something that's public knowledge but she's wrong in one respect. It can't just be anyone's blood. It has to be mine. Or of one of my people."

'adad was staring at us both opened mouthed. "Wait... Are you trying to tell me you can travel in time using the stone circles and standing stones as well???"

"Not just in time," laughed Bran. "With the standing stones you can travel in space as well. If you know how to do it, you could travel from here and now, to your village, the day or the week, or the month BEFORE the Romans attacked. They can take you any-where and any-when. That's where we messed up. The stones are a natural evolution of the Circles but what we didn't anticipate was that they would be capable of taking you anywhere, anywhere at all. In time or space... Even different realities. All it takes is the knowledge and a little bit of blood. An offering if you will. You need to pay the toll."

"Aaaanyway" I continued... "Getting back to our story..."

I wasn't being deliberately rude. Yes, I know I am perfectly capable of it but if I left this up to them, then we'd still be here chit chatting as winter drew in.

"...The following day we arranged to meet up and tour the cup and ring marks, there's currently a project going on, from Edinburgh Uni' or some such place, to digitally record all the cup and ring marks in the Glen"

Bran snorted "Good luck!!"

I smiled in agreement. "When we got to the top of Achnabreac she just completely lost the plot. She became all angry and irrational. I tried to distract her, but she literally just dropped me through time. One minute I'm trying to defuse the situation when there was a pop. Like when your ears pop? I literally blinked and when I opened my eyes, I was stuck waaaaay way back in time. Back even further than we are now and with absolutely no idea where I was, how I'd got there or how to get home. Oh... and whilst I remember... What is the story with the amulet? You know, that thing that you gave me that I've been using as a key ring?

Bran dutifully produced the evidence. "You do know how dangerous it was for you to make this don't you??" he said reproachfully.

'adad sighed. Taking the amulet in his hand, "I made it to try and save your grandmother's life. You know, I presume, or you've been told of the side effect of travelling in time? That you no longer age? Well, that's not strictly true. If you stay in the one time for long enough then eventually age catches up with you but the moment you start travelling again it stops. I guess it's like a mechanism or something to allay suspicion, you know, if you've been away from home for years and years and then return to the same point in time, it's so you don't look like you've aged 3 years when you've only been gone for three minutes. If you see what I mean." I nodded. "Anyway, your gran died of cancer. This was the third time she had been diagnosed with it and this last time she refused treatment. That first time? I was terrified. It had been eating her up inside for months and there was no sign that the treatment was even working. That's when the idea came to me. I thought if she came with me... If we started travelling, then it would stop the cancer. Shed stop ageing. More to the point, she'd stop dying. She understood exactly what I was trying to do but she refused. Said one lifetime was enough and that she was content with the one she'd had. When the cancer went into remission, we spoke no more about it. I never mentioned it the second time, I even considered letting the museum have it but you'd always loved it and so I gave it to you. The third time I was desperate and brought it up. We fought. God how we fought."

He lapsed into silence, and I took a hold of his hand. Lending him the strength to carry on. His eyes met mine. "You have to believe me, I tried to tell her, persuade her. We could have travelled together, I could show her things she could never imagine, we could have had more time together, but she refused. In the end there was nothing I could do. My last words to her were words of anger." He looked at Bran, "do you have anything to drink.?"

I laughed. "In this place? Of course he does. I'm not entirely sure, but he could probably give you whatever you wanted to drink. From anywhere in time or space."

"Jen... Shush." Bran said, disapprovingly, as he handed 'adad a glass of water.

Taking a long drink, he continued with his tale. "Once she had gone, things started to change. I started having dreams. Memories of things and people long gone started to haunt my waking hours and then one morning I woke up and I knew. Something had happened. Time had been changed. It was at that point that I knew what I had to do so I sorted out my affairs, packed my bag and left. I left the Glen. I left you and the rest of the family, and I left the amulet. Content that it would just remain a curiosity, a key ring, more than likely lost in the bottom of your drawer or the back of your locker."

He paused before turning to look at me "Is that how you ended up back here? How Beira managed to throw you back? You had the keyring with you when you went up to the circles?"

"Yes and No..." "Interrupted Bran. "You see, Jen appears to have a natural ability to use the circles. I have a feeling that given the right set of circumstances Jen would have fallen through time anyway. Luckily the Amulet masked that ability from Callie for a while. At least long enough for Jen to learn how to use the Circles and get used to defending herself. Something which I hear she managed quite effectively in their last confrontation."

Dammit it ...!!! How does he keep finding these things out??

"For some reason, which I have been unable to fathom, not only can Jen use the circles, but she can harness the power which accumulates therein. Even though thus far, all of the occasions when she has used it have been entirely on impulse. It is through the agency of this vast source of power that she was able to change time. Subtle, it was not, though I'm sure she could get better with practice. The noise that resulted in such a vast discharge of energy, was felt all up and down the corridors of time."

"But how is that even possible?" 'adad was aghast.

"It's actually your fault." Bran smiled. "Mine!? How could it possibly be my fault? I kept it all a secret. All of it. I never even told Ian, my own son. Jen certainly never knew."

"As it happens" Bran explained, "Jen's blood, and by extension, your own, is quite a bit older than either of you realise. In fact, it goes all the way back to the very first of your people who learned the secret of the circles."

Suddenly 'adad was on his feet... Striding about the clearing...

Blood!!!!

"That's what she wants... That's what she needs!" He looked at Bran. "She needs your blood. She needs your knowledge, and she needs Jen in order to change time and here we are, gathered together in the same place at the same time like lambs to the slaughter. Both of you should go!!! She can't be allowed to go back and change everything."

Bran shrugged off the revelation. "She can need my blood all she wants, but I think she will find the taking of it more difficult than even she realises. Not to boast but I am most likely immune to harm from any of your modern weapons. Steel will no more harm me than iron, or bronze..."

A grim smile crossed 'adads face. "What about a stone knife...?"

The smug look fell from Bran's face, to be replaced with a look of genuine concern. "That could probably do it. In fact, that would probably do it quite well."

It suddenly dawned on me…

See??? I'm not completely oblivious to everything that was going on round about me.

…I turned to 'adad. "The knife I pulled from the stone!!! She said it was almost identical to the one which you had loaned the Museum years before.!!! I subsided, confusion clouding my mind. "But if it's the same knife, then how could it be in the museum and wedged into a rock at the same time??? How could it exist at the same time, in the same place and be both broken and in one piece…"

Bran rolled his eyes… Ok… Let me explain. Pay attention, I don't want to have to do this more than once. Nothing gives me a headache quite like having to explain temporal mechanics. What has undoubtedly happened is this; at some point, between now and then, Callie, who currently has in her possession, the intact knife, which was donated to the museum by your grandfather, will jump back to a point in time, somewhere between now and then and will wedge it into the rock, to be retrieved, broken, by you, over the summer holidays in 2019. One would assume that if you hang about here long enough then sooner or later you shall both be reunited with your murderous ex-friend."

A voice interrupted his lecture… "I do so much prefer sooner…. Don't you?"

Chapter 19

It was her. I would recognise that voice anywhere. She stepped forward into the circle of light cast by the fire.

"Hello Jen, I see you managed to survive your little trip through time, something tells me you've been quite busy since our last little get together." She pulled off her rucksack and sat down on it. Regarding us each in turn. Her eyes rested on Bran "You I don't know, but you," she turned to 'adad. "You, I remember very well indeed. Hello Maelgwyn, it's been a long time."

"I haven't gone by that name for hundreds of years Beira… Or is it Callie now?

She shrugged. "Either will suffice. It has been many years since I gave names any consideration. They come and they go. Some last longer than others. Callie was a name I was particularly fond of. I couldn't for the life of me think why I had chosen it, but it occurs to me now that my subconscious must have remembered a young girl, way back in time, who used to call me that."

I was sitting staring at her when there was noise outside the light cast by the fire. Immediately she was on her feet, as calm as she appeared, she was obviously wound tighter that a lute string. I glanced at Bran just in time to see him frown and shake his head, with one finger he slowly traced a golden spiral in the air and vanished. I understood why he had gone. Callie could not, under any circumstances, be allowed to acquire even the tiniest drop of his blood, but still, I can't deny I was more than a little bit annoyed that he just up and left me… Left us to deal with Callie on our own.

Of course, it was the very first thing she noticed when she returned. We finally managed to persuade her that he was just the local hermit and he had run off into the night, scared for his life. Which left just us.

The joys

"Why are you here Beira? I am old now and don't have it in me to fight you anymore."

She laughed… "You? You think I came back here for you? Oh, my dear fool. As she has probably told you, your granddaughter and I have a bit of history and one morning, after I had cast her adrift, I awoke with a head full of new memories. Memories of specific events which differed substantially from that which I knew had occurred, so I gathered what I needed and decided to return to the scene of the crime as it were. And who do I find, sitting here quite the thing, but my old comrade in arms and his erstwhile granddaughter. One big, happy, family reunion. I tried to kill you once my friend. I won't miss a second time. And if someone," she glanced at me. "Gets in my way, then I am perfectly happy to get rid of your granddaughter whilst I'm at it. It makes no odds to me. One of you is good. Two is undoubtedly better."

'adad had started to his feet at the matter-of-fact way in which she was calmly discussing our murder. "There's no point in harming the girl, she's only here by accident after all, it's not like she could do you harm, not someone as experienced as you."

She giggled…

I kid you not. she actually giggled. There was definitely a rise in the level of crazy in her voice.

"My dear boy, you seem to forget, I can remember what she did that night in the field over there. I can remember what she did as clearly as you. And more to the point, I understand the implications of that, more than you ever will. I have travelled and seen things you can only dream about. I have lived lifetimes searching for the answers that I needed and everything I've learned points to one thing. One indisputable fact. It takes something more that human to change time. So, tell me, Maelgwyn. Was it you? Did you marry outwith the family? Or was it maybe your son?" He stared at her in silence, she shrugged. "It matters not, someone somewhere in your ancestry dabbled with someone who was not quite in the same gene pool. As a result of whatever weird genetics now infuse her cells, your granddaughter can actually change time. And that," she paused, "is exactly what she going to do for me."

For the first time I actually laughed. "You must really be crazy if you think there's anything you can do that will persuade me to help you. After what you did. After the people you've killed…"

She had drawn a knife from her belt. Not just a knife. The knife and she was sitting tapping it thoughtfully against her cheek as she stared at me. "You will help me, 'cause if you don't, then I will kill your beloved 'adad. Slowly. Painfully."

'adad snorted, "She's going to try and kill me anyways whatever you say Jen"

"Of course I am" she said cheerfully. "But if she helps me then maybe I won't make her watch as I do it"

OK… I think that's a confirmed case of total batshit crazy.

"Sooooo, what's it to be Jen??? We could travel together, it'd be a lot of fun. You and I, together, travelling in time. Having fun. It'd be just like old times. We could totally get the band back together. You always said you loved history, well, I can take you places and show you things that you could never read in a textbook. All you have to do is either show me how you did it or come along with me and lend me your… Expertise. What do you say? You and me? Road trip?"

"You're actually serious, aren't you?? I was completely incredulous"

"Oh, I know we've had our differences but that's in the past now… Or is it the future?" Again, that bone scraping giggle sent shudders through my body. "We'll be like sisters. It'll be fun!" Blood was starting to drip down her face from where she was obsessively tapping the knife, it gave a demonic look to her face which wasn't helped by the eyes. The last time I had seen eyes like that was right before she had thrown the baby into the fire. She was staring at me with frightening intensity.

"Come with me Jen. We can do this together. Come with me." her voice had developed a kind of sing song quality which, I'm pretty sure, wasn't a sign that things were getting better. In fact, things were starting to get well out of hand.

Suddenly Callie lunged forwards as if someone had hit her with a two by four. Emerging from a fold in the night came Bran, brandishing a staff.

Huh… I guess he didn't abandon us after all. Who woulda thunk?

She spun round. I wouldn't have credited that anyone could move so quickly. The sound, dear god the sound, that issued from her mouth was almost feral in nature. The snarl on her face betraying nothing but rage. I moved before I had time to consider the consequences, the only thing in my mind was "get the knife." 'adad had drawn her attention away from Bran who showed no sign of following up his attack with any sort of meaningful action. 'adad had started moving even before me and was now face to face with Callie. Locked in a dance that only had one possibly conclusion. Neither could afford to turn away, neither willing to stop…

It happened so quickly that I almost missed it. Bran moved. That was all it took. The briefest moment of inattention from Callie and 'adad lunged at her, desperately she turned her attention back to the dance and threw up her hands. The coming together had all the finality of a gunshot and I understood instantly that one of them would not be getting up.

Silence filled the clearing. I could feel my heart beating in my chest, the blood flowing in my veins. I was praying to whatever god was listening. Please 'adad, please get up, over and over in my mind. My thoughts and prayers stretching into the endless now. Then it started.

The giggling.

The laughing.

I could feel parts of my life shutting down as she rose from the ground like a scene from my worst nightmares. I desperately tried to tear my eyes from the sight which consumed me, from the body that lay crumpled on the

227

ground. It couldn't be him. It just couldn't. Not when I'd only just found him again. It couldn't be him... He wouldn't leave me. He couldn't leave me. And through all these thoughts the laughter just went on.

Blood.

It was a potent thing. A symbol. For all of human history it had been deemed as special and it wasn't until this night that I really understood why. I could feel it. With every beat of his faltering heart more spilled out onto this sacred ground. I could feel something inside me stir, echoed by something in the earth. Something fed by the life flowing from my grandfather. Sacrifices had been committed here. Sacrifices to old dead gods. Forgotten by the people. Forgotten by history but the land? The land remembered...

I could feel power gathering. Undirected. Uncontrolled.

Looking for a vessel to fill.

Looking for me.

Magic.

It flooded into me, burning through my body. Searing along the new pathways which had been burned in my mind. Wild, untamed magic, desperate to escape, to manifest, but I held on. I don't know how, but I held on. It was more seductive than I had ever felt before, swirling through my mind and body. Inviting me to take it, to use it, to give in to it. My control was tenuous at best, but somehow, I managed to hold on.

I could see her now.

Standing over the body.

Circles and Stones

Laughing.

The last thing I heard before I let go, was Bran.

"Jen... Don't..."

My willpower dissolved in a burst of heat. My entire being was being consumed by light and fire. I had found my purpose and had given myself over to it completely. Time itself surged through my veins, speaking to me, informing my actions... Showing me an endless multitude of futures and an infinite number of pasts. Every single one focussed on me in the here and now. I felt it fill me to the brim and with nowhere else to go it burst out of me. I looked at 'adad. I could bring him back. I could bring any of them all back. Aoife. 'adad. Gran. I could reach across that barrier and bring them back, but as soon as the though occurred, I knew that it could not be. Bowing my head I knelt and touched his face, absorbing his past, his present and his future. Seeing everything he had been, everything he could have become. The years wasted. Her.

I pulled the knife from his chest, the blade slicing into my hand as I did so. The power flaring as it came into contact with my blood. I could feel... Could almost hear the stones humming, but without Brans blood, or the blood of one of his people there was no way out. No way for it to activate.

I bore down on Callie, her death in my eyes. I could see any one of a hundred ways in which she could die. Each one as pointless. Each one as futile. Each one worse than anything I could possibly do to her here and now.

Bran had come up behind me and reached out, grasping at my shoulder. He pulled back with a gasp as if burnt... "Jen... Oh my god... What have you done? You need to let it go… This could destroy you… So much power was never meant to be held by one such as you… You need to let it go!!"

"No!!!" I screamed. I turned to face him… I could see the blood drain from his face. I don't mean he went white, I mean I could actually see it. The blood in his veins. The beat of his heart. I was connected to every single thing in this glade. In the glen. I could feel them all. All that power just flowing into me. "She needs to pay!"

He was staring, "Jen… Your eyes…"

I learnt later that my weird eyes were burning like molten gold.

At that moment, a movement caused me to spin, my blood scattering ruby droplets through the air, each one burning with crimson fire...

My blood.

Red droplets scattering from the tip of that cursed knife. Callie was still here. Still unwilling to submit, then, like a wounded animal she threw herself at me.

Once again, just as it had on the night of the naming, time seemed to slow… I could see her hanging in the air… I could see my blood, arcing through the night to splash against one of the stones.

Blood spilled.

My Blood.

The moment it hit the stone the humming rose to a scream and the night sky was torn asunder... Time and space twisting in on itself…

"How...? How did you...?" Brans voice, shouting into the silence of my mind... "What have you done Jen? How could you do this? You can't do this! It's not possible!!!"

All of this happened in the time it took for me to blink. Callie was still coming at me, her face transformed into a mindless mask of hate, arms outstretched, hands like claws. For the first time, she looked like her namesake. The Cailleach. The Hag.

With a thought I slowed time to a crawl, searching in my newly expanded consciousness for the answers I needed. It only took a moment. Absorbing. what I needed. Learning between the ticks of the clock and with one last look at her hated face I opened a portal right in front of her. Given our history together, I figured this was the least she deserved. One good turn deserves another.

The power I had released was slowly slipping out of my control. The maelstrom threatening to pull us all in. An irresistible, invisible wind pulling at us. My eyes were fixed on the spot where my blood had landed... The spiral glowing with a blinding light. I pushed my way towards it, struggling against the wind.

I knew what I had to do.

I knew what needed to be done.

With the last of my strength, I focussed everything I had into the hand holding the knife. It blazed like the midday sun as I swung my arm down and plunged the stone blade into the spiral. The surge of power was staggering. I felt the handle of the knife flare and turn to ash in my hand and with a last surge it was over.

Darkness.

Everything was darkness.

I could hear stone creaking and popping as they cooled from the onslaught of the inferno I had unleashed. Even the rocks of this place had barely survived...

Oh god... Bran!!! 'adad!!!

In the centre of an untouched piece of grass sat Bran cradling my granddads head. I pulled myself to my feet and walked unsteadily over to where they sat. "Is he...?" Bran nodded. "I'm so sorry Jen, he's gone." I nodded and slumped to the ground. Drained. Numb to everything that had just happened. I had no idea where I had sent Callie. Hopefully far enough away in time and space that she would not be troubling us again. I closed my eyes, taking 'adads hand in mine, feeling for the first time that he was truly gone. That he was truly dead.

It was over. Finally. I would grieve later. Everything in its proper time.

I sighed and lay back on the grass, staring at the night sky. Time... Everything always came down to time.

Living. Dying. There would be time enough for all of it. I'd made sure of that. Maybe, if I was lucky, at some point there would be time enough to go home.

Home... It sounded odd in my ears. Maybe later, there was still so much to see. Still so much to do. There would be time enough later. There would always be time for one more trip...

******

We carried 'adads body back to the cairn and laid him with his beloved Aoife, then, for the second time in 24 hours I stood in silence as Bran commended someone I loved to the care of their ancestors. In his hand I placed the amulet, one side now burnt and partly melted, thus bringing everything full circle.

"Soooo..." I sighed, looking at Bran "What now?" He'd avoided really talking to me since we'd left the stones but now, he looked at me, concern etched on his face

"I don't know Jen. You could go home, it's there, waiting for you." He paused.

I could totally hear a but coming...

"But there's something in you. Something which I have felt stirring, something that awoke fully last night and which you obviously have little or no control over. I'm not sure that letting you go home is the responsible thing to do. You could hurt... Hell, you could kill yourself... Or your family. From what I saw here, tonight, you could accidentally wipe your entire village out of history.

I was stung by his criticism... "I thought I managed all right, I did kinda save us all. In case you didn't notice!"

He stared at me, his eyebrow doing that thing. "But was that you using the power... Or was that the power, using you?

I started to answer, tried to deny it, but I couldn't. I could remember being shown... Being directed... The feeling of joy at being unleashed... A feeling that wasn't mine. I knew he was right... "So..." I asked again. "What now?

"You stay with me. I teach. You learn. And in between times we'll hunt for Callie. Or you could go home. I won't stop you if that's what you wish."

He was right. And it's not like Mum and Dad would even miss me. Ha! I'd only been gone for like five minutes after all.

I looked at him, taking in those eyes which so curiously mirrored my own... "I guess we should probably get started..."

<u>Afterwards</u>

Callie opened her eyes to darkness… Golden eyes stared down at her. The face, too beautiful to be human receded into the darkness and a voice rang out... "Nuada!!! She wakes!!!"

End

K. Baxter

<u>Appendices</u>

<u>Notes on translations</u>

There are so many side benefits to travelling in time, the whole not aging this is the most easily brought to mind. Understanding languages being another, but just like the ageing thing, once you return to your own time it slowly starts to fade. That which was so easily acquired is just as easily lost. Turns out if you really want to learn Gaelic, or Brythonic or any other language for that matter then you need to put in the time. And the effort. It's a long process but I guarantee it's worth it. I've been kinda busy and my Gaelic is a bit rusty, so you'll hopefully forgive me if the translations aren't quite up to what you'd expect from a High Priestess.

I jest. Honest.

I'm going to add just a wee note here as to the pronunciation of certain names. As I said earlier, it's really bad form to get someone's name wrong all the time and these people are my friends and family so making sure you say their names right is the very least I could do.

OK.

Aed: like the Aed in Aedan. Simple enough

Circles and Stones

Aoife: Ee-Fa

Balach: Pronounced as written. The ch at the end is like the ch in Loch

Beira: Bee-ra

Caoilin: Kay-lin (or Quail-lin)

Eithne: Ayn-yuh (or Enya)

Gwenhwyfief: An attempt by Aed to Gaelic-ise my name. Don't @ me, I love it.

Maelgwyn: Mail-goo-win. You know? Now that I see it, I guess its not such a huge stretch to get from this to Malcolm.

Ruairidh: Roo-ry

******

Adding on to that, you may have noticed a smattering of Gaelic throughout this account. Below are translations to those various little bits and pieces that I've sneaked in throughout the book. Just to tweak your interest you understand. However, for those of you who don't have an internal google translate I will aid you in your quest for knowledge.

Chapter 1

Theirig air ais!!: Go Back!!

Theirig air ais agus dùsgadh!!: Go back and wake up!!

Chapter 2

In which my dad mutters:

Dia cuidich mi" at me. Basically, this is asking for divine intervention. "God help me."

So, this was where it all kicked into high gear, and I started waxing lyrical in Gaelic. Without even knowing it would you believe. I'm kinda peeved at that. An accomplishment like that and I woulda quite liked to have known about it. Showed it off a bit you know? Never mind. It all started with Hilary calling me:

Amadan Ruadh! (That is essentially red-haired fool)

And me responding with:

Caillie bhan!! Radh a-rithist!!! Even now I'm kinda proud of that one. It just kinda rolls off the tongue. In a nutshell what I said to her was "Say that again you blonde haired hag!!"

And that seems like as good a place as any to draw the curtain down on this chapter of my adventures.

Circles and Stones

K. Baxter

Sneak Peek of Book Two.

The Wytches Stones

Chapter 1

We'd been at it for 6 weeks, 6 weeks of rain and mud and jaggy bushes. We were almost finished damnit! All it would have taken, would have been another week and we would have been done. Unfortunately for us, it had been at this point that the government had woken up to the danger of the pandemic which was raging across Europe and put us all into lockdown.

Which meant, goddess save me, that for like the next 4 whole I had been trapped in the house.

You have no idea.

My mum.

My dad.

And me.

This was not a recipe for good times

But last week, all of that had changed. Last week, lockdown had come to an end. Rumour had it that we would even be going back to school.

No... not the same school. They had refused to take me back, even though I had grown my hair. Even when I had solemnly promised to be a good little drone. Hell, even when mum had gone into full-on meltdown in the rector's office.

I know, right?

As a result, I'd started at the academy in Stirling. After the summer holidays when we'd returned from my somewhat extended break in Kilmartin. As far as my parents were concerned, we'd spent just over seven lovely weeks in the glen. I however had spent a little bit longer...

5 years longer

5 years, slipped in between the passing of one day to the next.

I was a changed woman. My mum quietly attributes the change in my attitude to the shock of being expelled from school. "Maybe that will teach you" was her current favourite. I however put it down to the fact that inside, I was actually 21 years old. Not the 16 years which were on show to the rest of the world.

A minor, if handy, benefit of travelling in time.

It had taken me a while to get back into the swing of things. Hot running water. Coffee. The internet. All of it seemed so unnecessary when I came home. No... Not home. As awful as it sounds this place no longer felt like home. Home was a small stone built cottage in a place and time far removed from this bustling city. Home was Aed and Caoilin and Balach.

Enough. I'm not here to fixate about the past.

Ha! Who am I trying to kid? Everything I did was focussed on the past.

With the end of lockdown, it signalled a return to what had become my lifeline. My Passion. Upon returning to the 21st century I had become involved with the Rock Art Recording people

We get out, and we look for instances of rock art. You know.... Cup and ring marks. Petroglyphs.

Circles and Stones.

Ok... Now do you get it?

They were in the glen last summer? Recording and mapping rock art. It turns out they were busier than that. Turns out they were at it all over Scotland and there was a group in my very own back yard as it were. So... given my extensive experience and my newly discovered ability to find them. Find isn't really the right word... its more... I don't know how to describe it. That I can FEEL them is about as close as I can get to explaining it. It's like a tickle inside my head. Anyway, it seemed only fair that I should avail them of my expertise.

I had learned alot last summer and I faithfully promised my teacher that I would practice. 'Natural ability is all well and good but if you don't practice then the abilities will fade Jen.' That's what he said. My Teacher I mean; Bran. It had been months since we'd talked. In fact he had been completely silent since I'd returned. I hate to say it but I really missed having him around.

I digress.

What I'm trying to say is that last year I had learned the secrets of how to use the stones. And the circles. I know, It's not the most accurate of descriptions but I clung to it because that's what we had called them. My grandad and I. Circles and Stones.

The upshot of the matter was, that this weekend, I was going to be onsite with the Forth Valley team recording an extensive example of Rock Art on the other side of the hill. Not only that, but this time we were being joined by the Professor.

This woman had written the book on rock art...

And I mean that quite literally. She wrote the actual book. Remind me later and I'll dig it out for you.

If you want to know about rock art? This was the place to start.

Well... If you want to know what academics thought it was all about. If you wanted to know what they were really for... Best just stick with me.

Ok. So now that your all caught up.

I was currently on my knees. In the dirt. Brushing leaves and stuff away from the cup and ring marks. This one in particular was HUGE. I mean. Usually you get a cup, maybe a couple of rings. Very rarely do they exceed 12 inches across but this one.... 9 Rings. 26" across. This thing was bigger than any I had seen since leaving the glen. The workmanship wasn't great, The outer ring was a bit shoogly but all in all it was hugely impressive. I'd have to compliment Bran if I ever...

No... Not if. WHEN I saw him again. Already, last summer was taking on the appearance of a dream. After all we had been through... Everything we'd seen. Everything that he had taught me I thought he might have at least kept in touch.

But no. Nothing. My inner Bran had even ceased to be, the moment I'd stepped back into this present.

As was always the case when I lose focus whilst working on site, I began to hear the sound. Like the after effects of a giant bell.... I realised I had been tracing my fingers round the biggest circles and it had begun to hum under my hand.

"It's quite impressive, isn't it?" The voice startled me, and I turned to see the smiling face of the Professor. I jerked my hand back quickly. Guiltily. "I was just... thinking the same thing. About how impressive this one is. The smaller rings, the cups, all of it combine to make this one of the most impressive that I've used... Found!

Found.

Damn it... I really need to stop doing that. Someday, someone was going to notice.

"You've seen a lot then?"

"More that you'd think" I laughed, I seem to have a knack for finding them, but I've seen nothing on this scale since I left the Glen. Kilmartin Glen I mean."

"Of course!!" A smile split her face. "You must be Jen. I have heard all about you. The ones you found in your village caused quite the stir, but thanks to you they are now in the official record. They are some of the most unusual ones I have ever seen." Very different in character to these or the ones further west."

I smiled then. "They were most likely just done by a different artist" Even as I said it a shiver ran down my spine. A different artist. Someone other than Bran. Would you believe that thought had never actually occurred to me? There were hundreds and hundreds of these scattered all over the country. It would be insane to assume that Bran had carved them all. Hell, he'd basically said as much. It had been so much easier when I could just bloody ask him about these things. I slapped my hand down on the rock in frustration.

By the way. Slapping your hand down onto a hard surface. Such as rock. Hurts. Seriously. One of these days I would learn.

The moment my hand came into contact with the carving is when everything went sideways. The circle was suddenly alive. Alive to my touch. Alive in my mind. The shock of it numbed my arm. The pins and needles biting into my skin. That in itself would have been enough to make me swear. I didn't, but it was close. However, what was even more inspiring of profanity were the words and the voice which echoed in my head the moment my hand touched down.

"Call me."

Call me? Really? 8 months of silence and I get "call me?

Bran had finally made contact.

K. Baxter

Copyright © 2022 by Kenneth Baxter

Printed in Great Britain
by Amazon

84801359R00150